WHEN HEARTS COLLIDE

LORANA HOOPES

DEDICATION

Dedication Page:

To my family who allows me to sacrifice time with them to write these stories.

To my friends who inspire me even when you don't know it.

To women everywhere who have been attacked or forced to do things against their will, your Heavenly Father loves you.

Thank you so much for picking up this book. I hope you enjoy the story and the characters as they are dear to my heart. If you do, please leave a review at your retailer. It really does make a difference because it lets people make an informed decision about books. Below are the other books in this series. I would love for you to check them out. I'd also like to offer you a sample of my newest book. Free Sample!

The Heartbeats series:
The Power of Prayer

Where It All Began

A Past Forgiven

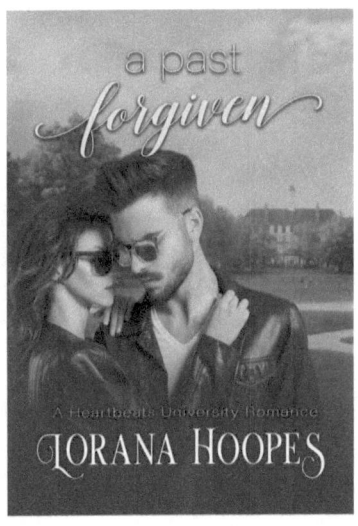

ear covered Jared like a blanket. The music that had been uplifting now pounded a drum of dread in his heart. Why did it have to be so loud? He pulled desperately on the arm of a nearby boy, spilling some of his beer. "Where's Amanda?" The boy rolled his eyes, cursing a little at his spilled beer, and shrugged Jared off.

Jared turned to another, who gave the same response. His heart pounded like a freight train as his eyes tore wildly around the room. He had known this was a bad idea. Frat parties were often dangerous, this one even more so.

The crowd of bodies pressed against Jared, surging to the beats of the pulsing music. Sweat from those around him joined his own, trickling down his back. He pushed against the crowd, fighting his way to the other end of the house where the bathroom and bedrooms lay. He had to have taken her to one of them. A hand grabbed Jared's wrist, and he whirled on a blond surfer type with long hair.

"Sorry, bro," the surfer dude said, holding his hands up in apology.

Jared continued toward the back. A tipsy blond fell into him, and he shoved her to the side. The bathroom door loomed just ahead.

"Amanda?" Jared pounded on the white wooden door. "Amanda, open up if you're in there." The pounding of his heart was now reverberating in his head, creating a headache that made his eyes hurt.

The lock clicked, and the door opened. A thin brunette in a miniskirt and crop top stumbled out. "There's no Amanda here." Her words were a slur, and her brown eyes barely focused on him.

Jared grabbed the girl's thin shoulders and shook her. "Have you seen her? Red hair? She would have been with Caleb West."

The girl shook her head and fell into the wall as soon as Jared released her. Rolling his eyes, he pushed past the girl and opened the first bedroom door. A couple was entwined on the bed, but the girl had blond hair and the face of the man didn't belong to Caleb.

"Sorry," He pulled the door shut and moved on the next one. Another couple was heavily involved on this bed too, but again no Amanda.

The next door was locked. This had to be the one. Jared rattled the handle, but to no avail. "Amanda?" He pounded on the door, but he heard no noise from inside. Jared grabbed the arm of a nearby male and pointed at the door. "Hey, can you open this? Do you have the key?"

"Sorry, I don't live here." The man shrugged and walked away.

"Aargh!" Jared turned back to the door and rammed his frame into it. The door didn't budge. Perhaps a kick would work. He took a step back and planted a perfect front kick. He felt the reverberation up his leg, but not even a tremor from the door. Cursing under his breath, Jared looked around for anything to wedge in the door. Would they have a crowbar in the house? Would anyone have one in their car?

"Jared!" At the sound of his name, Jared whirled around. Emily was fighting her way to him through the crowd. Thank goodness, she had seen the text. A glance at his watch revealed ten minutes had passed since he had texted her when he'd first lost sight of Amanda.

"Have you seen her?" Emily asked when she reached him.

Jared shook his head, the fear constricting his vocal chords. "Not since I texted you. I saw them at the punch table and then a friend came up to me and started talking. When I turned around again, she was gone. It's my fault."

"It's not," she said, running a hand through her long blond hair. "You warned her, and that was all you could do."

Jared wasn't sure about that. He should have pushed harder. He should have told her the whole story and not just part of it, but none of that made a difference right now. Right now, he needed to find her. "I've already checked those two rooms," he said pointing to the previous doors, "but this one's locked."

Emily glanced around, but like Jared, her search came up empty. "I'm assuming you already tried hitting the door," Emily said, "but what if we tried together?"

"It's worth a shot," he said. "On the count of three, okay?"

Emily nodded, and on the count of three, they

both rammed the door as hard as they could. This time the wood did tremble, but the door remained locked.

"Again," Jared said through clenched teeth, and together they rammed the door once more. This time a wonderful terrible splintering sound of wood echoed, and the door opened. Jared rushed into the room.

Amanda lay sprawled on the bed. Her shirt was open and her pants were undone, but still on.

"Check on her," Jared yelled to Emily as he scoured the room for any sign of Caleb. The closet was empty, but a chill crept in from the open window. Jared stuck his head out, but the area was dark and devoid of movement. If Caleb had gone out this way, he had gotten enough of a start to be out of sight. Without knowing which direction he had gone, trying to follow him would be pointless.

With an agitated sigh, Jared turned back to the bed. Emily had wrapped the comforter around Amanda, whose eyes were wide open and filled with fear.

"Can you move?" Emily asked. No head shake, but Amanda's eyes moved left and then right. "Okay, it's going to be okay. We'll get you out of here. Any sign?"

"No, the window is open, but he's gone." A tear slid out of Amanda's eyes. "Don't worry, we'll find him. He won't get away with this." Jared patted her hair tenderly and wiped the tear from her cheek. Then he scooped her up and headed back out the door. "Let's get her to the hospital."

"An ambulance is on its way," Emily replied, pocketing her cell phone.

Jared nodded as he pushed his way through the crowd. A few people turned to gawk at them as they made their way to the front door, but most were oblivious and kept dancing to the loud beats or tipping back their drinks. Jared shook his head as disgust boiled inside him. What was wrong with these people? Did they not even care that someone had been attacked?

The night air slapped him as they exited the stifling house, and the change in temperature sent a shiver down his spine as the cool air licked up the wet sweat dripping down his neck.

The ambulance roared up moments later. The EMTs climbed out and took Amanda from Jared, strapping her onto a gurney. As they loaded her into the back, Jared climbed in.

"There's only room for one," the EMT said as Emily attempted to climb in too. "Besides, the cops want a statement." He pointed to the police car pulling up.

"Go. I'll stay with her, and when you're done, we can switch," Emily said.

Jared nodded and mouthed a silent thank you to Emily as the doors closed. He grabbed one of Amanda's hands and sent a prayer heavenward. *Please God let her be okay, please God.* He had no other words, and hoped God was hearing his heart, which felt like it was beating out of his chest. Though he'd only known her a few months, Amanda was a friend, and if he were honest, he hoped she would become a lot more.

When the ambulance braked, Jared fell forward a little. Chilly air rushed in as the back doors opened and doctors took over the gurney Amanda was on. Jared jumped down from the ambulance and hurried to keep up with them.

"Amanda? I'm Dr. Patrick, can you tell me what happened?"

"She can't," Jared spoke up. "I'm pretty sure she was drugged."

The dark-haired doctor turned to him. "And you are?"

"I'm Jared. I'm a friend, and I found her. Her

eyes were open and seemed responsive, but she couldn't even shake her head."

"Okay, we'll take it from here. You can wait over there." He pointed to the waiting area. Jared wanted to protest, but he could tell from the look in the doctor's eyes that his protest would fall on deaf ears, so he nodded and stumbled over to a gray, vinyl chair. As he sank down, the weight of the night descended on his shoulders, and he dropped his head onto his hands.

He hadn't been able to stop it. Was this what Nikki had gone through? Was this why she left without a word? Would Amanda do the same thing?

"Hey, are you okay?"

Jared jumped at the touch to his shoulder ready to lash out at the intrusion, but relaxed when the eyes he saw belonged to Emily. "Yeah, I guess I'm alright. How are you?"

Emily sighed as she sat next to him and pulled her knees to her chest. "I've been better. They asked me a lot of questions. I couldn't answer most of them, so they'll be looking to talk to you too. But I told them what little I could. How is she doing?"

"I don't know," Jared sighed. "They whisked her away pretty quickly and haven't been back out yet. I'm worried, Emily."

"I am too," she said with a nod, "but the best thing we can do right now is pray." She took his hand, and they closed their eyes. "Father, our friend Amanda needs your help right now. Please be with her and give the doctors the knowledge to treat her. Lord also help us know how to help her in the future."

As they said amen, Jared added a silent plea for Amanda to be okay. If she wasn't, he wasn't sure he'd ever be able to forgive himself.

CHAPTER 2

 wo Months Previously

AMANDA ADAMS STARED at the tiny gray room and sighed. This was going to be her new home away from home at least for the next year, and it was rather depressing.

"Well, it's got a lot of potential," her mother said with a false brightness as she looked around. Amanda raised her eyebrows. Potential? Maybe for a horror movie. Boring white walls dotted with myriad holes boxed the room in. Two small brown dressers with two drawers each separated two bare mattresses on metal frames.

Rolling her suitcase into the room, Amanda

hoisted it onto the left bed and shivered at the groaning cacophony of creaks that answered back. She crossed to the right bed and pushed on it, hoping for a better outcome, but a similar noise resounded. "Right. Potential."

Crossing her arms, she emitted another sigh and surveyed the rest of the room. Two small closets framed either side of the doorway. One wall held a small sink and a vanity with a cloudy mirror. Two study desks took up the remaining space.

"Come on now. I know you can't paint the walls, but you can hang pictures, right?"

Amanda nodded. "We just aren't supposed to put holes in the walls, but I guess that's not a hard followed rule," she said as she glanced at the holes that contradicted her statement. "I don't think I brought enough with me though to cheer this up."

"So, we'll go shopping and get some more pictures. With your bed made up and some bright colored towels, it can at least look a little more 'homey.' And we're only a six-hour drive away, so you can come home on long weekends or we'll drive up."

"Yeah, I guess you're right." Amanda crossed to her suitcase, unzipped it, and began removing the clothes while her mother grabbed a towel and began cleaning the cloudy mirror. Suddenly, the door slammed open. Amanda dropped the shirt she had been holding in surprise and spun around.

A girl with long black hair shaved short on one side and a nose ring entered and narrowed her eyes at Amanda. "Who are you?"

Amanda swallowed and stepped forward, extending her hand. "I'm Amanda. I guess I'm your roommate."

The girl rolled her eyes and pushed past Amanda, ignoring the hand. "Crap. I told them I wanted a single."

"Oh, um, well maybe they ran out," Amanda stammered as she dropped her hand. The hair on her arms bristled at the girl's brusque demeanor. She looked to her mother for help, but she just shrugged.

The girl flung her backpack on the right bed and glared at Amanda. A chill ran through Amanda at the girl's icy blue stare. "Well, I'll be asking them to look again. I don't do roommates." She rifled in her backpack for a minute, turned and glared one more time, and then abruptly left the room, slamming the wooden door for a second time.

Amanda stared at the closed door and blinked. "Well, this should be fun."

"Maybe they'll change her room after all."

Though the words were positive, her mother's voice was filled with doubt, mirroring Amanda's own.

"I can only hope." Amanda returned to the job of unpacking and when she had finished, she locked the door and followed her mother to her mother's car. They had driven up in two cars, so Amanda would have a vehicle to drive home in if necessary.

As they walked around the local Wal-Mart filling the cart with fun pictures and colorful towels, Amanda couldn't help thinking that it still wasn't going to be like home. She wasn't going to have many of her own things. There would be no brother and sister busting in while she was trying to study or Kate rattling on about the latest trends as they quizzed each other. And if that girl remained her roommate, it was going to be an uncomfortable year regardless of what she hung on the walls.

When they returned to the dorm, Amanda opened the door cautiously in case the mysterious, angry roommate was there, but the room was empty and looked exactly as she had left it. Taking the pictures out of the bag, along with the poster putty, she began hanging them over the bed she had chosen. Her mother cut the tags off the towels and hung one by the sink and placed the others in one of the drawers beneath it.

Amanda finished hanging the posters, stepped off the bed, and surveyed the room again. While it still didn't feel exactly like home, it did feel warmer than when she had first arrived.

"Are you sure you're going to be okay?" her mother asked, pulling her in for a hug.

Amanda rolled her eyes goodnaturedly as she hugged her mother back. "I'll be fine. You have to let me grow up sometime, Mother."

"I know, but I didn't think it would happen so soon." She wiped a tear from her eye and then pulled Amanda in for another hug. "Come home as often as you need to, okay?"

"Okay, Mom." After another few awkward hugs, Amanda finally ushered her mother out of the dorm room. As the door shut and the silence crept in, she turned back to the bed and sighed. She had hoped that she might meet another girl like Kate, someone she could relate to, but this roommate, whatever her name was, didn't seem like she wanted to be friends at all.

Rifling through her backpack–the only thing she hadn't completely unpacked–Amanda pulled out her Bible and prayer journal and sat on the squeaky mattress. Though her prayer journal was just a spiral notebook and not a nice leather bound one like Sandra's, it accomplished the same goal, and she'd had it since joining Sandra's prayer team three years ago. It was nearly full now, and she was excited about the prospect of having to get a new one soon.

Amanda flipped to the last entry and dug a pen out of her bag. On the next available line, she added 'patience to deal with my roommate, and the words to say to reach her.' She tapped the pen against her teeth as she thought about what else to add. 'Wisdom in how to further God's plan here.' Having no idea what God had planned for her at the university, she figured she should leave the request broad and just listen for his wisdom.

After closing the cover, she set the journal beside her on the purple bedspread. Then she picked up the Bible and flipped it open to John where she had last been reading.

As her fingers touched the page, she smiled. No matter how many times she opened it, the Bible always transmitted a feeling of peace and happiness. It had ever since she was a small child. Her mind drifted back to the day her father had led her in accepting Jesus as her savior.

"If you are ready for God to come in your heart, you just repeat after me," he said.

Amanda nodded at him. She wanted nothing more than to know this heavenly father he spoke so highly of.

"Father, I know I have sinned," he said.

"Father, I know I have sinned," she repeated.

"But I also know that you died to save me from my sin, and I want you to rule my life."

She repeated the statement and immediately felt a warmth wash over her. With wide eyes, she looked up at her father who smiled.

"You felt it, didn't you?" he asked.

She nodded.

"Good, now the next step is to know all there is about God. You can never learn enough. In fact, how about we start reading the Bible together and when you get old enough, you can read it on your own and we can discuss it?"

She nodded, eager to read with him. He pulled her onto his lap and opened the important black book to the beginning.

"Genesis Chapter 1," he said. "In the beginning, God created the heavens and the earth."

And that's what they had done. Amanda had been a precocious child and an avid reader at the tender age of five, but the Bible's vocabulary had been a little challenging until she was older. Even when she could read the words herself, she still didn't always understand the concepts, so he had set up a chart of the books with a point system, and she had earned points for every book she read and could discuss with him.

In this way, he helped her understand the parts she missed as they discussed it. Then she could trade the points in for treats. She had never told her father, but she would have read the books for free, partly because she loved learning about God and partly because she always looked forward to those discussions with her dad. He was often busy with work, but he always made time for her in the evenings when she wanted to discuss God.

At ten, he had baptized her, even though he wasn't the pastor. He had been a deacon of the church at the time though, and they had agreed he could. Amanda had only grown from there, telling everyone she met about Jesus and his love for them. It hadn't always been easy, especially in a public school where Christianity was frowned upon, but God had helped her stay strong, lead several friends to Christ, and helped her form a Fellowship of Christian Athletes at her high school last year that she hoped was going to continue just as strong this year.

Propping the pillow up, Amanda leaned back against the wall and drew her knees up to serve as a stand for the Bible. As she scanned the page for where she had stopped, the door flew open again and "the roommate" entered, stopping short at the sight of Amanda's open book.

"Oh gaud, you're one of those?" Disdain dripped from her voice.

"I'm sorry, one of what?" Amanda placed her finger on the spot she had just found and looked up at her.

"One of those Bible beaters." The girl's nose wrinkled in distaste as an ugly sneer crested her face.

Amanda chuckled and smiled. "I am a Christ follower, if that's what you mean."

The girl rolled her eyes, mumbled something under her breath, and pulled out a pair of headphones. She plugged them into her phone and then turned up her music.

Flinching at the loud beat that escaped the headphones and filled the room, Amanda turned back to her Bible, trying to block out the noise. The words jumped on the page as she tried to focus, and after reading the same sentence four times, she decided to finish her devotional later. As she closed the book, her stomach rumbled. Food sounded like a much-needed distraction.

Though Amanda hoped the girl would decline, she figured it would be rude not to at least invite the roommate, since they were going to be spending a lot of time together. She waved her hand to get the girl's attention. The girl rolled her eyes, but pulled one headphone back. "I'm going for some food. Would you like to come?" 'The roommate' flicked her hand in dismissal, and relief flooded Amanda's body. Grabbing her key and ID card, she hurried out of the room before the girl changed her mind.

A dingy brown carpet ran the length of the hallway. Though Amanda had known the dorm hall was old, she had hoped maybe the university would have spruced it up some. Identical brown doors lined the hall and a set of stairs sat at either end. Amanda headed to the right and down the flight of stairs, which opened to another hall on the first floor. Though nearly identical to the second floor, an information desk filled some real estate directly across from the front entrance.

A mousy girl in glasses sat behind the desk, her nose buried in a book. Rows of mailboxes sat open behind her.

"Hi, can you point me in the direction of the cafeteria?" Amanda asked as she approached the counter.

The girl's eyes flicked up briefly. "We don't have one here. You'll have to go to Bledsoe-Gordon Hall." Her eyes dropped back to the book.

Amanda took a deep breath and clenched her teeth against the snippy reply trying to escape her mouth. Was everyone at college going to be this rude? "Okay, it's my first day, though, and I seem to have misplaced my map. Do you have another one?"

The girl turned and grabbed a piece of paper off a counter behind her. She held it out, never looking up from her book. It must have been riveting.

"Thank you." Amanda took the paper and sat down in one of the chairs near the counter to peruse it. Her eyes scanned the rectangles for the words 'you are here.' When she found them, she placed her finger there and read the names of the closest buildings to find Bledsoe-Gordon Hall. Sneed Hall, Doak, West, ah there it was Bledsoe-Gordon Hall. It certainly wasn't one of the closest buildings, but it didn't seem that far away.

Folding the map, Amanda placed it in her pocket, exited the doors, and turned left. Though Lubbock was, for the most part, flat and brown, the campus stayed relatively green, probably due to the sprinklers that ran incessantly. A few trees even popped up on the landscape though they were barren of leaves currently in the heat of late summer. Wishing she had remembered her sunglasses, she squinted and held up her hand as a shield until her sensitive eyes adjusted to the light.

Beads of sweat trickled down her back as she trekked across the grass. A few other people were out, most carrying boxes into other dorms, but some lounged at picnic tables reading or chatting with friends. Oh how she wished Kate had come to Texas Tech with her, but she couldn't begrudge Kate's choice to go to the same college her brother was attending. After nearly losing him to a drug addiction, Kate had wanted to be closer to him. Still, it would have been nice to have her best friend here with her.

Bledsoe-Gordon came into view, and Amanda turned up the cement steps. As her hand reached the silver handle, the heavy door flew open, knocking her down the steps and onto the jarringly hard ground. Her head flew back and her teeth snapped together, sending a pain across her jaws and down her neck.

"Oh, sorry are you okay?" a male voice asked.

Amanda shook her head to clear the stars and struggled to stand. Gritting her teeth, she blinked back the tears threatening to spill out from the throbbing of her rear end and head. Gingerly, she rose to her feet, dusted off her backside, and focused on the man on the steps.

Close cropped blond hair framed a ruggedly

handsome face. His eyes were the color of the ocean, and his nose had a chiseled-from-stone appearance. A grey t-shirt covered his broad shoulders, showing off his muscular arms and chest. His waist narrowed, and under his shirt, he wore tan cargo shorts. Brown flip flops finished off the look, giving him a casual air.

"Sorry," he repeated. "I didn't see you there."

"Yeah, I got that," Amanda said. Though the stinging was subsiding, she knew she would be sore for a few days.

"Um, well hey, can I buy you lunch?"

"No, I'm fine, really." As she stepped past him, he grabbed her arm. Shaking off his hand, Amanda whirled, turning angry eyes on him. He stepped back, holding his hands up in defense. "Sorry," Amanda said, "but I don't even know you."

"I'm Caleb," he said sticking out his hand, "and I'm really not a jerk. Please let me buy your dinner."

Amanda cocked her head and regarded him. He appeared sincere, and surely there would be more people inside. "Okay," she agreed, smiling hesitantly and shaking his proffered hand. "Lead the way. I'm Amanda, by the way."

He flashed a charming smile and held the door open.

"Haven't you already eaten?" Amanda asked as they stepped in the hall.

"No, I live here. I was getting something out of my car for my friend."

"Won't he be wondering where you are?" The hallway in this dorm looked exactly like hers. Had none of these dorms been renovated recently?

"Nah, he'll be okay." Caleb led the way down the hall which opened into a large cafeteria at the end. Round tables full of students filled most of the room. The other side housed an assembly line where students could pick up food and then check out at the end.

After grabbing a sandwich, salad, and some fruit, Caleb and Amanda sat down at an empty table.

"So where are you from?" Caleb asked.

Amanda finished chewing the grape she had just popped in her mouth before answering. "I'm from Mesquite; how about you?"

"Houston. I can't say there's much to do here, but at least it isn't as muggy."

She nodded, remembering her trip to Houston in High school. Kate's aunt had lived there and one summer Kate had asked Amanda to go with her. The heat had hit as soon as she de-boarded the plane, flattening her red hair to her forehead in a sticky mess. To cool off, Kate's aunt had driven them to the neighborhood pool, but even the pool water had been so warm that they had been forced to sit in the hot tub first before jumping in the pool to at least make it feel colder.

"So, what are you studying?" Caleb asked before taking a bite of his sandwich.

Amanda narrowed her eyes at him, unsure how much information she should give out to a perfect stranger, even if he was a ruggedly handsome perfect stranger. "Counseling." She decided to keep it vague until she knew more about him. "What about you?"

"Business right now, but I'm not sure that's where my passion lies."

"What do you think you'd rather do?" she asked. Her counseling instinct had kicked in, sensing that there was a story behind the slight sadness of his statement.

"I think I'd rather be an architect." His blue eyes sparkled as he spoke, and her heart flipped and began beating faster. "I always loved building things, even as a kid."

"So why aren't you going into architecture?"

His face fell, and his shoulders sank. "My dad," he sighed, "He really wants me to go into business with him, but he owns a furniture store, and I just can't see myself really happy running it."

She nodded, knowing that feeling all too well. Though her own family had always been very supportive of what she'd wanted to do, she had known a girl in high school who had wanted to pursue acting, but her parents' desire was for her to become a lawyer. The girl grew so stressed every time "the future" was brought up in class that she had given herself ulcers. "It's not my place, but your career is the rest of your life. I think it would be hard to do something you're not passionate about."

"You don't know my dad," he said, shaking his head.

She shrugged. "I know, that's why I said it probably wasn't my place, but I do think sometimes as much as you want to please your parents, you have to do what's right for you. If it helps, I'll pray for you." Amanda stuck a grape in her mouth and watched for his reaction, hoping he wouldn't be offended by the offer to pray for him. He was intriguing, and she wanted to know more about him, but only if he were open to God.

"Thanks, I'd like that," he said.

Amanda smiled, and they finished the rest of dinner in a companionable silence. "Well, it was very nice meeting you," she said, standing and placing her trash on the tray. Caleb stood as well.

"Can we meet up again?" he asked.

Amanda bit her lip even as her heart fluttered. Should she give him her number? Though she didn't know him, he appeared genuine, and she could always use new friends in this unknown territory. Plus, it was just a number. It wasn't like she was going to jump into a relationship with him. Even if he was handsome, that wasn't her style. Curiosity tamped the small amount of trepidation, and she agreed. They exchanged cell numbers before saying goodbye, and then Amanda headed back to her dorm.

The dark cloud wasn't in the room when Amanda returned, but her essence remained. This was going to be a long semester.

CHAPTER 3

*J*ared Masterson unlocked the Students for Life office door and checked the answering machine. No calls yet, but it was only the first day of the new school year. When the parties started and people began hooking up, there would be many messages on the machine. While he loved being able to help people make a choice once they were in a bad situation, he wished there was something more proactive they could be doing to keep students from getting in those situations to begin with.

After he finished getting the brochures in order in case anyone visited, he pulled out a chair and sat down at the small conference table. From his backpack, he withdrew his Bible and placed it on the table. He tried to start each day praying that God would send them the people they needed to reach.

"Lord, use me today to do your work. Help me to see the people that need help and to have the words to say to them. And Lord, please send us new members to help spread your word this year. Amen."

As he ended the prayer and opened his eyes, he flipped to the back of his Bible and removed the photo he kept there. Though a little faded, the girl's green eyes and bright smile still touched his heart. His finger traced her face, and he wondered again if she were okay.

Nikki had been his girlfriend last year for half of the year until she met Caleb. Then, all of a sudden, she had decided she and Jared were no longer compatible and had broken up with him. Jared was crushed but had accepted her decision. Near the end of the school year, she had disappeared. Dropped all her classes and left without a word to anyone. Jared wished she had come to see him before she left or contacted him after. He just wanted to know she was alright.

"Still haven't heard from her?"

Jared glanced up to see Emily Peters throwing her gym bag in a chair across from him. Her blond hair was tied back in its usual ponytail.

"No," Jared said with a shake of his head. "Has she contacted you?"

"Sorry," Emily said as she sat down, "but we weren't that close, so I'm not surprised."

"Do you think he's still here?" Jared asked.

"Caleb?" Emily snorted. "Probably. He's a big man on campus here. Why would he go elsewhere and risk not being number one?"

"I hope we can stop them this year," Jared said, frustration boiling up inside him.

"We don't even know they did anything, Jared," Emily said, placing her hand on his arm. "Nikki could have left for a lot of reasons."

"You didn't know her like I did," Jared said. "Something happened to her, and I guarantee you Caleb West or one of his friends was involved."

THE BLARING ALARM elicited a sigh as it went off. Rubbing her eyes, Amanda glanced at the clock on her cell phone. Ugh, 6:30 was way too early. What had she been thinking taking the eight am classes? She loved learning, but it sure had been nice getting to sleep in all summer. With a final yawn and stretch, Amanda pushed herself to a sitting position.

Sunlight was barely filtering in the window, and across the room, "the roommate" was still asleep. Amanda still didn't know her name. As quietly as she could, Amanda pushed back the covers, crawled out of bed, and crossed to her closet, which sat on the right side of the door. After pulling on a pair of jeans and a light blue top, she brushed her teeth in the small sink and ran a brush through her hair, laced up her sneakers, and stuffed her backpack with the books she would need for the day. Grunting, she hoisted the heavy bag on her shoulder and quietly closed the door behind her.

The hallway was still dark as the lights in the hallway didn't give much light and there were only the windows at each end to let outside light in. Amanda took the stairs down, careful to hold the railing as the stairwell was even darker.

The bottom floor was lighter as it housed the front door and the administrative desk. Sitting down in a chair near a light, she pulled out her map. Her first class was in the math building all the way across campus. Second was History in Holden Hall and then Psychology back down by the dorm. At least all the classes were close together; even if they were on the other side of campus from her dorm.

Refolding the map, she pocketed it and pushed

open the front doors. The cool morning air dispelled the last edge of sleep and invigorated Amanda's spirit. Though it would get hot later–one hundred was forecasted today–right now the temperature was seventy-one and perfect. The sun wasn't out just yet, but she patted the pocket of her backpack to make sure she had her sunglasses. She would need them later. The familiar bulge eased her worries as she began the trek to Bledsoe hall.

Very few people were out yet, and the quiet was almost unnerving. The birds chirping was the only sound. Even the sprinklers were silent this early in the morning.

Amanda couldn't help wondering if she would see Caleb at breakfast. They had exchanged numbers, but it was too early for him to call, and she wasn't going to call him first. Still, he was a face she knew, and it would be nice if he were there.

The cafeteria was sparse as Amanda entered. Only ten or twelve students dotted the tables and Caleb was not one of them. She chose some eggs and pancakes from the buffet and scanned the room. The choices were to sit alone or join someone at a table. Most students were immersed in their cell phones, but one blond girl in an oversized shirt sat alone, picking at a waffle. Amanda decided to try to be friendly.

"Hi, can I join you?" Amanda asked, setting her tray down.

The girl looked up, sadness emanating from her eyes. She shrugged, and then her eyes dropped back to her plate.

"Um, I'm Amanda. First year." Amanda hoped the girl would at least respond; she had no idea what the girl was going through, but her counseling instinct wanted to help. If only she'd had more experience. What she'd been able to do at JD's clinic hadn't been much, mainly filing paperwork and discussing vague scenarios with the actual counselor.

"I'm Jordan," came the mumbled reply, "Sophomore."

"Nice to meet you," Amanda pressed, but silence met her back. Jordan continued to push her waffle bits around on her plate. Her pale and splotchy face made Amanda wonder if she'd gotten any sleep the night before. "Are you nervous?"

The fork stopped, and Jordan looked up. Icy blue anger replaced the sadness, and Amanda shivered as the eyes bore into her own. "No, I just don't want to be here, but I couldn't afford to give up my scholarship." With that she grabbed her plate, stood up, and walked away.

With a sigh, Amanda loaded some eggs on her fork. Her first day was off to a stellar start.

AS THE LAST CLASS ENDED, Amanda gathered her books and returned them to her backpack. It was time to head back to the dorm and tackle some of the massive pile of homework she had been assigned today. Funny, she didn't remember anyone warning her about homework on the first day or how much there would be. She was going to have her work cut out for her.

The bright sun blinded her as she pushed open the door of the building. Squinting, she reached into the pocket of her backpack and pulled out her sunglasses. While she loved the color of her green eyes, she often wished they weren't so sensitive to the sun, but that was an inherited trait from her father. At least she didn't need them for vision like he did. She could still hear him complaining about how the tint of the prescription glasses never got quite dark enough for him.

As the dorm came into view, Amanda whispered a silent prayer that "the roommate" wouldn't be there. She knew that wasn't very Christian of her, but the girl was such a downer, and Amanda just wanted to decompress after the first day.

The same mousy brunette was manning the front desk as Amanda stopped to check for mail; her face was still buried in the book.

"It must be good," Amanda said teasing her.

The girl glanced up, annoyance in her eyes. "Did you need something?"

"Um, just the mail for room 216, if there is any."

The girl turned, scanned the rows of slots, and shook her head before sticking her nose back in the book. Amanda nodded and started up the stairs, the mantra "please be gone" repeating in her head.

The door to the dorm room was shut, but that meant nothing. Holding her breath, Amanda turned the knob. Locked. Well, that was probably good. Fishing her key out of her pocket, Amanda unlocked the door and pushed it open. The room was dark, quiet, and blissfully empty. Sighing, she shut the door and dropped the heavy bag on the creaky bed. Then she pulled out the mountain of homework and spread it out at the desk.

It wasn't taxing work, really, but the quiet settled on her shoulders creating an unnerving sensation. At home, her little brother and sister would have been constantly interrupting her. As Amanda thought about them racing around the kitchen, loneliness set in.

On the first day of school last year, she and Kate had gone out for pizza and then walked around the mall. They had met up with a few other friends and the group had spent most of the year together. Though a small group, they had been close knit, and Amanda had always been surrounded by a great group of friends. Now, she had no one really.

Sighing, she stood up from the desk and crossed to the bed to retrieve her Bible. As she opened it, she searched for the source of comfort that usually accompanied it, but today nothing hit her. Her mind was not focused. With a sigh, Amanda returned it to the nightstand and decided to take a walk.

Amanda grabbed her sunglasses, locked the door behind her, and trudged back down the stairs. One thing was for sure, she was going to be in great shape after this year. As she stepped into the warm sunshine, her phone buzzed in her front pocket. Kate's number flashed across the screen, and she eagerly swiped the screen.

"Kate, how are you?"

"I'm good," she laughed. "How are you?"

"I'm okay, I guess. I miss you." Amanda crossed the grassy lawn to a nearby tree and sat down against the trunk. The rough bark bit into her back, but she didn't mind. Her best friend was on the phone.

"Uh oh, what's wrong?"

"I'm just a little lonely is all. My roommate is a nightmare, and I tried to make a friend this morning, but I don't think it went over well. I feel a little out of my element." Amanda hadn't meant to unload on Kate, but the words just fell out of her mouth.

"I get it. I have my brother, but we don't have any classes together. We got together for dinner last night, but he seems so much better I'm not sure I made the right decision coming here."

"Sounds like we both had unrealistic expectations," Amanda sighed. "I did meet a guy though."

"Ooh, do tell."

Amanda smiled at Kate's teasing tone and filled her in on the meeting of Caleb.

"He sounds hot," she sighed, "when are you going to see him again?"

"I don't know; we exchanged numbers, but I think I should wait for him to call, right? I don't even know the rules of dating." Amanda had been on a few dates in high school but none of them had panned out, and she'd been too focused on her grades to pursue any further.

"Yes, you should wait for him to call. You don't want to seem too eager. Oh crud, my roommate just returned and wants to get an early dinner. Can we talk again later?"

A hint of jealousy flared in Amanda's heart. How come Kate was given a roommate she could befriend while Amanda had the still-unnamed epitome of anger as her roommate? With a shake of her head, Amanda pushed the un-Christian thought away and hung up the phone, not sure if she felt better or worse. She pocketed the phone and pushed herself up from the grass. Might as well finish the walk.

After the walk and a dinner by herself–Amanda didn't feel like trying another awkward conversation–she returned to the dorm room. The roommate was sprawled on her black bedspread leafing through a magazine. She looked up long enough to roll her eyes and then returned her focus to the magazine.

Amanda stared at the contrast in the room. Her side of the room was bright and cheery while the girl's side was dark and monochromatic. Resolved to try to befriend the girl again anyway, she pulled back her shoulders and took a deep breath before asking, "How was your first day?"

The girl snorted in response, and a flicker of annoyance sparked in Amanda, but she swallowed it down. God obviously had a reason for pairing them together. Had she prayed for patience lately? She couldn't remember, but this situation would definitely be a way to practice it. "Can you at least tell me your name? I'd like to call you something other than 'the roommate' or dark haired girl."

The blue eyes rolled again. "It's Jade, but don't get attached. One of us will be leaving soon."

"Or we could become friends," Amanda tried.

"Doubtful," Jade replied and jammed the headphones that had been lying around her neck into her ears.

Amanda shook her head and grabbed her prayer journal. She had told Sandra she wanted to stay a part of the prayer team, but she hadn't been able to get the weekly requests before leaving Mesquite. Checking her watch to make sure it wasn't too late, she pulled out her phone and dialed Sandra's number. "Hey Sandra, it's Amanda Adams. Are there any new prayer requests?"

Sandra's voice on the other end was like a warm hug. After rattling off the prayer requests, Sandra filled Amanda in on the church service she had missed and asked how about her first day.

Amanda glanced at Jade. She didn't appear to be paying attention, but Amanda didn't want to chance it. "It was okay. Not as good as I'd hoped, but I know it will get better." She'd have to tell Sandra to add Jade to the prayer list the next time she called. "Be sure to say hello to Callie, JD, and little Hope for me," Amanda said as the conversation ended.

"Are you really going to pray for all that?"

Her eyes flicked to Jade who had obviously been listening and was now staring at her with one eyebrow raised. "Of course I am. These people need God's help."

"Why don't they just ask for it then?"

"They do," Amanda said with a smile, "but there is power in prayer, so more people praying can only help. Besides it keeps me connected to God."

"And what if God doesn't answer your prayers, what then? Won't you just have wasted all that time?"

Though the questions were snarky, Amanda wondered if they were laced with curiosity as well. Although people claimed to be agnostic, she had never met one who truly was. Most people either didn't know God or had been wronged and therefore hated God.

"It's never a waste to pray, and God answers our prayers every single time. We just don't always like or understand the answer."

Jade removed her headphones and sat up. "What do you mean?"

"I mean people always expect God to give them things, so they pray for money or cars, things like that. God does give us those things occasionally, but sometimes what we ask for isn't good for us. God always has three answers to prayers: Yes, no, or not yet. See, he has a plan for all of us, and while we don't know exactly what it is, he does. He answers in ways that will glorify that plan. We won't always understand his answers, but we can know he's always listening and watching out for us."

"That sounds stupid." Jade rolled her eyes and replaced her headphones. She laid back and rolled over to face the wall.

Amanda sighed as she reached for her Bible. Jade must hold the Guinness World Record for eye rolling, but something told her that the girl fit into the "had been wronged and was blaming God" group. Amanda clearly had her work cut for her and would need God's divine intervention.

CHAPTER 4

*A*s the first week ended, Amanda's loneliness settled ever deeper. She had spent every breakfast, lunch, and dinner eating alone after the disastrous breakfast on the first day. Classes hadn't been much better, as she hadn't met anyone she could connect with, and then there was Jade who seemed determined to try her patience every chance she got. Amanda wasn't used to not having friends, and while she wanted to be strong, she was contemplating driving home for the weekend just to see some familiar faces.

Amanda glanced at Jade who was scowling at some book she was reading. She seemed even grumpier than usual though Amanda had no idea how that was possible. Still, they were both alone, and they both needed to eat at some point. Maybe Jade would come to dinner with her. Bad company at this point was more appealing than no company at all.

"Hey Jade, I'm going to go get some dinner. Do you want to come with?" Amanda asked, steeling herself for whatever Jade might hurl back at her. Jade didn't even reply, just continued to shoot daggers at her book. "Okay, well if you change your mind, I'll be at Bledsoe-Gordon, probably eating alone." Still nothing. Sighing, Amanda grabbed her phone and ID and headed out of the room.

As Amanda shut the door, her phone vibrated in her hand. She swiped the screen to see a message from Caleb. She had assumed he had either forgotten about her or just taken her number to be nice as she hadn't heard from him all week.

Want to grab some dinner?

Relief flowed through her at the thought of having someone to eat with, and she quickly texted back a yes.

True to his word, Caleb stood outside the door of Bledsoe hall. His blond hair sparkled like spun gold in the sun, and he waved as Amanda neared. Her heart fluttered and a heat crawled up her neck. She hadn't had a serious boyfriend in high school and wasn't used to the feelings flashing through her body.

"Hey, how was your first week?"

His smile blew away the darkness she had been feeling. "Everything was great, except my roommate. I'm pretty sure she hates me."

He laughed. "I think all roommates are like that at first. My first year, I had this guy, Owen, who played video games all night long. It kept me awake many nights, but it turned out he was lonely, so after we started talking, he stopped playing the video games and became a really great friend."

"Well, I hope things work out like that for us, but she appeared genuinely agitated that she had to share the room. I kind of doubt that we'll be bosom buddies anytime soon." Amanda's gaze dropped to the ground and she bit the inside of her lip. "I'm also feeling a little lonely if I'm honest."

Caleb placed a finger under her chin and pushed her face up until she was looking in his eyes. "I can't imagine you being lonely, but I remember my first year. It does get better. You just need to get connected. It's why I joined a fraternity my freshman year."

His eyes were so mesmerizing that Amanda

almost missed the word fraternity as it issued from his mouth. Her brow knitted together. He was a frat boy? The first inkling of doubt sprouted within her. She had heard stories of frat boys, and they weren't usually flattering. "I don't really want to join a sorority unless maybe it's a Christian one. Do they have those here?"

"I'm sure they do," he said with a shrug. "The bulletin board would be a good place to look. They have one in most cafeterias and at the student union. They're not all bad, you know."

"What?" Amanda asked.

"Fraternities and Sororities," he laughed. "I saw your face and heard the tone in your voice. I know we sometimes get a bad reputation, but I joined to connect with people. My fraternity doesn't even have the regular frat house, just a small place where we meet up once a week to catch up."

Heat seared across her cheeks as she stammered out an apology, "I'm sorry. I didn't mean..."

He held his hand up, interrupting her and smiling. "I was teasing you. Come on, I'll give you a quick tour of the most important places on campus before dinner."

As they walked around the campus, Caleb

pointed out buildings and filled Amanda in on other aspects of college life. She tried to stay focused on his words, but now and then her gaze would wander down to his mouth. He had perfectly shaped lips, and she couldn't help wondering what kissing them would be like.

She'd had only one kiss and it didn't really count. In eighth grade, there had been a game where you tried to pull the tabs off soda cans and keep them in perfect form. If you were able to, you could hand someone the tab and they had to kiss you. Rick, the pastor's son had handed her such a tab one day as they walked the church yard between services. Then he'd leaned over and kissed her lips. It had happened so quickly that Amanda wasn't even sure if it had been real or if she'd imagined it.

"Dinner?"

"Huh?" Amanda's face blazed at the realization that she hadn't been paying attention to anything but his lips.

He smiled. "I asked if you were hungry. Do you want to get dinner?"

"Oh, uh sure," she stammered, and then, as if on cue, her stomach rumbled, punctuating her words. *Could this get any more embarrassing?*

Chuckling, he led the way back to his dorm. The smell of marinara sauce wafted through the hallway as they entered.

It was Italian night, and Amanda piled her plate with spaghetti, garlic bread, and salad. Caleb grabbed a small lasagna and a salad, but no pasta.

As he led the way to a table, Amanda's brow furrowed. Did he know something she didn't? "Okay, seriously, is the food poisonous?" she asked as they sat down.

A melodious laugh flowed out of his mouth. "No, it's actually pretty good, but it's not often good for you. During my freshman year I packed on the dreaded Freshman fifteen and had to work extra hard to get it off. I've just learned since then that salad is usually safer, so I fill up on it and just take a small portion of the main dish."

Amanda was thoroughly embarrassed. *What must he think of me with my plate piled high?* "I'll keep that in mind," she said in a soft voice.

"No one told me either my first year," he said with a smile. "Hey, what's your schedule next week? I'd like to meet you after your classes if it fits with my schedule."

"You don't have to do that," Amanda said, but

even as the words left her mouth, her hand was fumbling in her pocket for the schedule as it wasn't memorized yet. Her heart raced at the thought of him meeting her after class though she tried to appear nonchalant.

"I know I don't have to. I want to."

The smile he flashed was pure gold and she reciprocated, feeling happy for the first time this week. She passed her schedule across the table to him, and he perused it silently.

"You have History near my last class, so I'll meet you outside your History class."

"Sounds like a plan."

After dinner, Caleb insisted on walking Amanda to her dorm. As the sun was setting, she agreed. The warnings of walking the campus alone at night had been drilled into her head before she graduated and then again at orientation.

The air was still warm as they crossed the luscious green campus, and the sprinklers were working late. Amanda's heart constricted when her dorm hall came into view as she didn't want the night to end.

Though the dorm had no strict visitor policy, Amanda wasn't ready to invite him in. She bit her lip, unsure of how to tell him that. Thankfully, Caleb seemed to read her mind and stopped outside the entrance.

He jammed his hands in his pockets, drawing her attention to his trim waist and the abs she was sure were chiseled underneath his shirt. Amanda forced her eyes to the side to avoid the heat she could feel crawling up her neck.

"Okay, have a good night, and I'll see you tomorrow," he said.

There was a moment of silence, and Amanda wondered if he were going to kiss her. Did she even want him to? No, it was too soon for a kiss. Again, as if seeing her thoughts, he leaned in and opted for a quick hug instead before turning back the way they had come.

Amanda watched him walk away, her nerves tingling at his touch. When he turned the corner and was out of sight, she entered the dorm and walked up the stairs. A dreamy smile played across her face. Even Jade wouldn't be able to spoil her good feelings tonight.

JARED SLAPPED the alarm off and rolled out of bed. Though he wasn't much of a morning person, he had found this was the best time to have his quiet time with the Lord. Grabbing his Bible from the nightstand, he sat at the small desk in the room and opened it up to Matthew 5, the last passage he had been reading.

"Lord, please help me be the light you speak of here. Use me to help reach others and share your word," he prayed as he finished the chapter. Then he shut the Bible and grabbed his shower caddy. Working at the Student Union wasn't his dream job, but it did put him in front of a lot people and allow him to be a witness to them.

JARED HAD JUST FINISHED BUSSING a table and was headed to the kitchen with a tub of dishes in his arms when he spotted the beautiful redhead. She had stopped inside the entrance and was scanning the area as if looking for something.

"Can I help you?" he asked approaching her.

When she turned to face him, his breath caught in his throat. Her green eyes were a bright emerald color, and her skin was a flawless porcelain. Jared hadn't been captivated by someone so instantly since Nikki a year ago.

"Um, maybe," she said with a shy smile. "I'm looking for the bulletin board where they post groups you can join."

He nodded and pointed to his right, "They are posted on that column over there. Are you looking to get involved in something particular?" *Please say a Christian organization.*

"I don't even know what they offer." Her smile stretched further showing off perfectly white teeth, "but I'd love to get involved in some sort of Christian club and a pro-life group if they have one. I know a lot of clinics closed with HB2, but now that it's been overturned, I just have this feeling they will be coming back."

Jared's eyes widened and his mouth dropped open. He had been hoping those very words would come out of her mouth.

"What?" she asked.

"Nothing," he said with a shake of his head. "It's just that I'm a part of Students for Life, the pro-life group here on campus. We're having our first meeting Friday night at Holden Hall."

This time her eyes widened. "Really? That is amazing. What are the odds?"

"Astronomical I'm pretty sure, if God weren't in control. This is a huge campus, and we aren't that big of a group. A lot graduated and even more stopped coming once the Planned Parenthood closed in town two years ago, but a core group of about fifty of us have continued, and we are always looking for new members. I'm Jared, by the way." He transferred the tub to his left hip and stuck out his right hand. "I don't always look like this, but I'm working today."

"I'm Amanda," she said taking his hand. A tingle shot up his arm at her touch, but he tried to keep his face from showing his excitement. He would have to get to know this girl better.

"I don't have a flyer on me," he said, "but I bet there's one on the column."

He led the way to the column covered with flyers for all the different organizations, and after a minute of scanning, he plucked a bright orange piece of paper off and handed it to her. "Here you go; all the information about us is on here."

"Thank you and count me in," she said flashing another bright smile. "I'll be there."

As she walked away, Jared turned his face heavenward and sent up a "thank you" prayer to God. He knew He'd had a hand in his meeting Amanda, and he hoped God had more in store for them.

AMANDA PRACTICALLY SKIPPED out of the Student Union. Not only had she found information about the two organizations she was most interested in, but she had a feeling Jared would become a friend. There was something in his hazel green eyes and comfortable smile that made her want to get to know him more.

The buzzing of her phone halted any further thoughts of Jared. Her heartbeat quickened as she swiped the screen to see a message from Caleb asking if she wanted to meet up. Her fingers flew across the on-screen keyboard as she typed out her reply and headed his direction.

"How are you holding up today?" Caleb asked when Amanda was within earshot.

"Better," she smiled up at him and then dropped her eyes. "It's nice to have a friend."

"I'm glad," he said, grabbing her hand and lacing his fingers with hers. "What would you say to a movie tomorrow night?"

He pulled her hand tight against his chest, sending Amanda's heart into overdrive. She could feel his heartbeat against her hand. She opened her mouth to agree, but then remembered the meeting at the pro-life group. "I'd love to, but I have a meeting I promised I'd attend tomorrow. Can we do it the next night?"

A hardness flashed in Caleb's eyes for a split second, but then he grinned, and Amanda told herself she had just imagined it. "Sure. What meeting are you going to?"

"It's a pro-life group here on campus. I want to check them out to see if they're worth joining." Amanda could barely keep the excitement from her voice. Then a new thought popped into her head. "Oh, hey, do you know of a good church around here? I need to get connected soon."

Caleb's brow furrowed and he glanced away, sending alarms bells sounding in Amanda's head. "Oh, um, I've heard of this place called Experience Life."

"You mean you don't go anywhere?" He had never explicitly told her he was a Christian, but Amanda had assumed from his actions and his letting her pray for him that he was.

"Well, I've wanted to,"–he stroked her hand and stared deep into her eyes– "but I get so busy studying, and I've never had anyone to go with me."

The bells grew silent as a fog descended on Amanda's brain, and a shiver ran down her spine. Of course, that made sense. She didn't like going new places alone either. "Well, will you go with me this weekend?"

"Ooh, I can't this week, but next week?"

Amanda nodded, disappointed, but next week was better than not at all, and she had asked him last minute. She shouldn't be surprised he had plans already.

"I have some items to attend to, but dinner tonight?" Caleb asked. "I'll text you when I'm done."

Amanda nodded and floated back to the dorm on cloud nine. Images of Caleb flashed in her mind–his blue eyes, his perfect smile. She couldn't wait to see him again, and after grabbing the mail, she took the stairs two at a time.

As she neared the room, she stopped and looked again, her forehead wrinkling. A sock was tied to the doorknob. Was this some sort of weird ritual that Jade had? Was it a prank? She had heard there were often pranks in college.

Amanda glanced up and down the hallway, half expecting someone to jump out of a doorway, but no one else was there. It didn't appear to be a prank. Shaking her head, she opened the door. Immediately Jade's head and the dark-haired head of some stranger popped up from under the covers on Jade's bed.

Her hands flew to cover her eyes, and her ears burned up. "Oh, my gosh, what are you doing?"

"Don't you know what the sock means?" Jade demanded.

"No, well I guess I do now. This is not appropriate. I live here too." Amanda hurried to her bed and grabbed her Bible off the nightstand. "I'm going to go do my devotion, and I'd appreciate it if you weren't here when I return, whoever you are." Keeping her hands as a shield over her eyes, Amanda tucked the book under her arm and left the room.

She shook her head as she shut the door behind her. It was barely the end of the second week and Jade was hooking up with someone. How could people do that? She had always been taught that intimacy was special and something you reserved for your husband. While television portrayed it as okay to jump in bed with everyone you dated, Amanda had been sheltered growing up and never been around someone who did it. Oh, how she missed Kate.

Leaning against the wall, Amanda pondered where to go. She couldn't very well sit in the hallway because eventually the man would be leaving, and she had no desire to see him again. She tucked her ginger hair behind her ear and took a deep breath, trying to slow the adrenaline coursing through her veins. She closed her eyes and racked her mind. Study carrels. There were a few downstairs. Maybe they would be quiet enough that she could do her devotion and get her mind off Jade.

The study room was near the right end of the first floor. It was like a living room, quaint with a few mismatched couches and chairs, a television, and a bookshelf loaded with books. Thankfully, no one else was in the room, so Amanda curled up in a cushy brown chair to finish her devotion.

She couldn't focus on the words though. Her mind kept wandering back to Jade. What must the girl be missing in her life to be so willing to jump into bed with someone so quickly? No advice jumped out of the book, but someone who might have some sprung into her mind.

Taking out her phone, she dialed Callie's number. Though Callie was probably busy with little Hope, Amanda could think of no one else who could answer the question better. Callie had once lived with a boyfriend until she ended up pregnant. After deciding to keep the baby, she had then began speaking to local teens about the importance of loving yourself and your body.

"Hello?" Callie's breathless voice came over the phone, and Amanda hoped she hadn't interrupted something important.

"Hi Callie, It's Amanda, do you have a minute to talk? I have a problem I'm hoping you can help with."

"Sure, I just got Hope down for a nap, so I'm all yours for at least half an hour."

"I just walked in on my roommate and some guy, and it's only the second week of school. Could she be using sex to fulfill some need that's lacking?"

"It does sound like she's compensating for something. Sometimes when people have sex that soon, it's because they've had it with so many people that they've lost themselves. They now have a piece of all those other people with them which makes finding themselves and being happy with themselves so much harder. Are you close enough with her to ask about her past?"

Amanda bit her lip, wishing she could say yes. "Not really. I'm pretty sure she doesn't like me, though she did ask me about praying the other night."

"That's a start. The best thing you can do for her is to try to be a friend and pray for her. I'll pray over here as well, and I'll tell Sandra to add her to the list. Oh, and one last thing. I'd pray for some wisdom. Anyone who uses sex as a coping mechanism is bound to end up pregnant before they're ready. She may have either had an abortion in the past, will have one in the future, or both," Callie cautioned. "Just be aware and ask God to give you the right words when you speak with her."

Amanda thanked Callie and hung up the phone. As she put the phone back in her pocket, her stomach rumbled, but she didn't want to carry her Bible all the way to the cafeteria if she could help it. She wasn't concerned about being seen with it but about spilling food or drink on it.

A glance at her watch revealed more than an hour had passed. Amanda had no personal knowledge of sex, but surely that was enough time to finish. Deciding to chance it, she headed for the stairs.

The sock was gone from the handle when the door came into view, but worry still resonated through her at the thought of opening the door and them still being engaged. Closing her eyes, she sent a silent prayer, turned the handle, and pushed the door open.

"He's gone; you can open your eyes."

Jade's sarcastic voice snapped Amanda's eyes

open. She stepped inside, still unable to look Jade in the eyes. Her eyes kept returning to the floor as if pulled by a tractor beam or a giant magnet.

"Have you seriously never heard about the sock before?" Jade asked as she pulled on a pair of black combat boots.

Amanda shook her head as she sat down on the bed. "No, I don't believe in sex before marriage, so I don't know all the code signs or lingo."

Jade stopped lacing her boot and stared at her. "You mean you've never had sex?"

"No, I'm waiting to do that with my husband. I've seen too many girls get pregnant or their hearts broken for one thing, and I want to follow God's command on the subject."

"Wow, you're really into this God thing, aren't you?" Jade finished lacing her boot and sat back.

Nodding, Amanda returned her Bible to its prominent place on the nightstand. "Yep, I've been a follower for thirteen years. He's always been there for me, even when people failed me." Something flickered across Jade's face. For just a split second, Amanda thought maybe her words had stirred some emotion, but then Jade's face hardened again.

"That's exactly why I stay away from God. I've

known too many Christians who sure didn't act the part."

"I'm sorry you had bad experiences," Amanda said softly, "but people aren't perfect, and they will often fail us. Only God is perfect. I try my hardest to follow his plan, but I still mess up. The difference is I apologize when I do, repent, and try to do better next time."

Jade's eyes locked with Amanda's. Could they be about to have a conversation?

"And you think that's all it takes? Just apologize and it's all good?"

Her words were filled with so much hate that Amanda could only blink for a moment. What had hurt her so badly in the past? "No, I... I mean yes, you apologize, but I guess it doesn't always make it better."

"It is people like you who turn people like me off. You live in your rainbow and unicorn world, where probably nothing bad has ever happened to you, spouting off trite words about repentance and forgiveness, but you don't know what it's really like. You've probably never had to hide in a closet hoping your stepfather won't find you and will give you one night off from being his punching bag or his play thing. I doubt your mom has ever forgotten you in her drug-induced stupor, leaving you to walk home five miles in the dark."

Amanda stared at her roommate. Was this her past? "Jade, I'm so sorry," she said.

"Save it," Jade said, pushing herself off the bed and storming out of the room.

Sighing, Amanda sent up yet another prayer for patience. "God, I'm way out of my league here, and I could really use some help." Her cell phone vibrated in her hand, and for just a moment she wondered if God was answering.

Opening her eyes, she read the message from Caleb. He was ready for dinner, and thoughts of Jade flew from Amanda's mind like leaves in a windstorm. A smile crawled across her face as she locked the door and jogged down the stairs to meet him.

"So, do you want to come up and watch a movie with me tonight?" Caleb suggested as they finished dinner and returned their plates and silverware to the kitchen.

The image of Jade and the unknown man in bed flashed before her eyes. "I don't think that would be a good idea," Amanda said, "but we can watch one down in the lounge."

Caleb's smile froze for just a moment. "Sure, I just thought maybe you'd want to be able to talk too."

"Well, are we talking or watching a movie?" Amanda asked with a laugh.

Caleb flashed another smile and led the way down the hall to the lounge. A big screen TV sat on the far side of the room. Next to it a shelf was teeming with movies. A few couches and chairs were set up around the room, very much like the study room at Amanda's dorm.

The room was empty, and Amanda paused. Would it be safe to be in here alone with him? She no longer trusted herself completely because new sensations coursed through her body every time they met up. There was no door on the room though, so she decided it would be safe enough.

Caleb picked out a romantic comedy and sat down on one of the couches. Amanda had hoped he would opt for two chairs, but swallowing her trepidation, she sat beside him.

Caleb opened his arm, clearly wanting Amanda to snuggle into it. She pursed her lips, trying to weigh the options. Deciding the pros outweighed the cons, she curled into the inviting open space. It was warm, comfortable, and the smell of his cologne reminded her somehow of home.

He placed his hand on her right shoulder and circled a slow pattern with his finger. A tingling sensation like nothing she'd ever felt before began bubbling in her stomach and crawling up her body, followed by a creeping warmth. Amanda snuggled deeper into Caleb's side, enjoying the masculine smell radiating from his body.

Her hand, seemingly with a mind of its own, found its way to Caleb's chest. The muscles tensed beneath her fingers, and the tingling sensation blossomed. Shifting slightly, Caleb cupped her chin and brought his soft lips down on hers. Amanda's breath caught in her throat as the tingling shot through her body, lighting up areas she hadn't even known existed. Her lips parted and Caleb's tongue touched her own. His hand edged under her arm, touching her side. An alarm began to blare in Amanda's head, and she pushed back on Caleb's chest.

"We should stop," she said, her breath labored.

Caleb turned his face away and ran his left hand across his face. "Of course, you're right. We should slow down."

Amanda nodded, but she hadn't been thinking

of slowing down. She had been thinking of slamming the brakes and putting the car in reverse. Red flashes of light had shot through her head, telling her clearly they needed to stop. "I should go." Caleb's face fell, pulling on her heartstrings, so she quickly added, "I'll see you tomorrow if you're free before my meeting, but I think we need some space tonight."

Before he could convince her to stay, Amanda rose from the plush couch and hurried from the room. Her body still pulsed with desire, and she didn't trust herself to stay strong.

As she hurried back down the main hall toward the front entrance, she hoped the air outside would be cool enough to tame the fire raging inside her, but it was still warm. Sighing, she forced her thoughts to something else, anything else, hoping to tame the flame that way.

Amanda's face still felt flushed as she opened the door to the room. Jade looked up and grinned a malicious smile. "Uh oh, did the goody girl get some? Not so high and mighty now, huh?"

"What? No, I didn't," Amanda stammered, "but I can see how people lose control now. And I am not high and mighty."

"It's not a big deal," Jade said, "It's a normal part

of life and yes, you are. You act like you are better than everyone with your Bible and your virginity."

Shaking her head, Amanda sat on the bed and grabbed her Bible for comfort. The textured black cover radiated calming waves as she held it to her chest, and her heart slowed. "I'm not trying to act like I'm better. I'm just trying to follow God's word. I know intimacy is a natural part of life, but it is supposed to be reserved for marriage. Otherwise, it becomes natural with everyone you date, and it loses its special meaning."

Jade shook her head. "There's nothing wrong with that, and *it is special* every time, believe me."

"Do you really believe that?" Amanda asked. She didn't want to sound preachy, but if sex was as special as Jade claimed, why was she always so moody? "Don't you think it would be more special if you really loved the person, and they loved you back? If you were in a committed relationship?"

"You don't know anything about me."

Her hard exterior was returning, and Amanda knew she was losing her. "Not for lack of trying. I've been trying to get to know you the last two weeks, but you keep throwing up walls."

"Whatever. We have nothing in common."

"We might. If you'd talk to me, we might find lots

in common. At the very least we wouldn't feel so alone."

"I don't feel alone," Jade said. "I have Gavin." And she turned back to her book.

Amanda stifled a small sigh, clasped the Bible tighter to her chest, and leaned back against her pillow. Jade was going to be a tough one, but she would keep trying.

CHAPTER 5

*A*manda swallowed the rather large lump in her throat as she dressed for the Students for Life meeting. Her nerves were jittering out of control. Jared had said it was casual, but the need to make a good impression weighed heavily on her heart. Her hope was that many of the people she met tonight would become friends. The Lord knew she could sure use some.

Deciding on a green shirt that complemented her hair, she pulled it and a pair of jeans on. After a final glance in the mirror and a quick fluffing of her long red locks, she left the room.

Even though the sun was setting, the air was still warm as Amanda crossed the green campus to

Holden Hall. As one of the oldest buildings on campus, it had a regal air, though the architecture of it wasn't as striking as several of the other buildings.

She pulled open the large wooden door and stepped inside. The smooth white floor contrasted the exposed bricks lining the inside wall. Research had informed Amanda that this hall had once been a museum, and she wondered how it must have looked then. A small white sign that read Students for Life pointed to the right, and she turned that direction, her footsteps echoing through the large hallway.

As she stopped in front of room 101, she took a deep breath before opening the door. Though large, the room was not as big as some of the lecture halls. There were round-tables and chairs set up about the room, and a small stage with a podium sat at the far front of the room.

Amanda wasn't extremely shy, but this scenario sent her heart racing. A sea of unknown faces stared back at her. What had she been thinking? A hand waved near the front, and she focused on it. It belonged to Jared and it felt like a life jacket in the unfamiliar water. While she didn't know him well, he was the only one she knew even a little. Squaring her shoulders and willing her nerves to relax, she pushed her feet forward.

"I'm so glad you could make it," Jared said as Amanda reached the table. One other guy and three girls were also at the table. "Guys, I'd like to introduce you to Amanda…. Sorry, I realize I didn't get your last name when we met."

Amanda's face flamed. "Oh, my gosh, I'm so sorry. It's Adams. Amanda Adams."

His green eyes twinkled as he smiled at her, and a calm flowed over her. What was it about him that made her feel so comfortable? "Okay Amanda. Well this is Chase, Sarah, Becca, and Emily," he said, pointing to each one in turn.

Chase reached out a hand first. He had dirty blond hair and friendly hazel eyes. His sharp features stood out on his clean-shaven face. Sarah's handshake was softer, though Amanda hadn't expected it with her steely eyes and hawkish nose capped off with spiky blond hair. Becca was a soft-spoken brunette with green eyes and a dusting of freckles across her nose. Emily came across as the sporty one in the group. Her blond hair was pulled back in a ponytail and the glistening of her face led Amanda to believe she'd either worked out just before or on her way here.

Though glad to meet new people she hoped would become friends, Amanda had no idea if she would remember all their names. She mentally went over them again as she sat down in the empty seat next to Jared.

The room quickly filled as others straggled in. A few came over to say hello to Jared and the others at the table. Jared was always gracious and introduced Amanda as well, and while she smiled and shook each person's hand, she knew she would never remember all of their names.

The sound of a hand tapping a microphone grabbed Amanda' attention, and she glanced up as a dark-haired woman stepped up to the podium. "Welcome everyone. I'm Tracy Martin, the president of Students for Life. I'll introduce the other officers in a minute, but I wanted to tell you all a little about what we do for the new people and a reminder for the returners.

"Last year we were mainly an educational group. We went to the fairs, and we distributed pamphlets about choices other than abortion. We will continue that this year. In fact, our first fair is next Monday. There are details by the door as you leave. I hope you'll sign up at the clipboard by the door, so we can contact you with future details of other fairs.

"As most of you know HB2, or House Bill 2, was repealed this year. This was the provision that made abortion clinics have to meet certain standards, and since most couldn't meet those standards, it forced many to close. We don't know what the repealing of this bill will mean yet, but I have an ominous feeling that it means more abortion clinics will be coming back. So, we are going to double our efforts this year. We may never get Roe v Wade repealed, but we can reach individuals and change their minds about abortion. We can show them the dangers of abortion and the humanity of the unborn."

Clapping erupted in the room. "Now, if I can ask the officers to join me up here, I'd like to introduce them."

"I'll be right back," Jared whispered and walked to the front. Amanda's eyes widened in surprise. She'd had no idea he was this involved. Sarah and Emily also stood and joined the group up front.

"This is Jared Masterson, our vice-president. Jared is a junior and has been involved with us since his freshman year. He's had a heart for the unborn ever since his mother told him she'd aborted a sibling before him."

Empathy tugged at Amanda's heart and tears pricked her eyes as she thought about her own siblings. She couldn't imagine knowing you should have a brother or sister, but that your mother had gotten rid of him or her.

"This is Emily Peters." Tracy continued, pointing to the petite blond. "She's a Sophomore and our Secretary. She'll keep notes of the meetings and send out emails if you miss them so you can stay up to date. Emily was adopted, so the sanctity of the unborn hits close to home. And finally,"–she pointed to the taller girl with the short blond hair– "we have Sarah Stewart. Sarah is a Senior and a communication major. She was conceived in rape, but thankfully her mother chose life. She'll oversee organizing events and putting the flyers together. We are all open to communication, so if you leave your email address on the sheet at the refreshment table, we'll be sending out our email and phone numbers to everyone."

Jared and the two girls rejoined the table, and Amanda's heart went out to him, to all the officers really. "I'm sorry about your sibling. I can't imagine what that must have been like. When did she tell you?"

"When I was fifteen, can you believe that?" he whispered, leaning forward, "She sat us down during a family powwow–I have a younger sister who was twelve at the time–and told us she'd gotten pregnant in college, but didn't want to give up her career, so she'd had an abortion. I asked her if she knew what the baby was, boy or girl, you know because I always wanted a brother, but she said she'd had the abortion too early to know. I don't know why, but it made me question if she really loved us. She tried to impress how important choice was, and that all children should be wanted. She made the baby sound like an inconvenience, and I told her that there were thousands of families waiting to adopt. I thought then, and I still do now, that she was being selfish. Our relationship has suffered since."

"Oh Jared, I'm so sorry. That has to be hard." Amanda had seen a few similar cases when she'd worked at JD's center. She still couldn't believe mothers would tell their children they had aborted a sibling, but the counselor on staff had said it was often the mother's way of processing their own guilt over the procedure. However, the news never sat well with the remaining kids as, like Jared, they almost always questioned why they were saved and not their brother or sister.

He shrugged. "It is what it is. It helped me find God. After that discussion, I was confused. I couldn't understand her, and it made me question everything. I found myself at church, and it was there I found healing. I pray for my mom every day to realize what she's done and repent, and I pray my sister doesn't follow in her footsteps. She'll be a freshman at college next year, and I know too well the temptations here."

"I'll add them to my prayer list too," Amanda said, laying a hand on his arm. "I have a friend who runs the prayer group at my old church. I'll have her add them to the list. We have at least fifty people praying every week."

Jared put his hand on hers and gazed into Amanda's eyes. A heat, starting at the point of contact, spread like wildfire up her arm, causing her heart to flip flop. "Thank you, I'd like that," he said. "Now, what's your story?"

"My story?" Amanda stammered trying to make her brain focus. She was having a hard time concentrating with his hand on her arm as it was sending her heart jumping. Why was his touch affecting her?

"This is my third year," he said. "Everyone has a story; some reason why they are pro-life and willing to fight for it."

"Oh," Amanda nodded, "Yeah, I have a story. My grandmother had a lot of physical issues growing up. When she married, the doctors told her she should never get pregnant, but she did. They recommended an abortion, but she chose to have the baby and my uncle was born. A few years later, my grandmother got pregnant again, this time with my mother. The doctors told her if she didn't abort my mother that she would die. If she had listened to those doctors I wouldn't be here, so choosing life is personal to me too."

"Did she die in child birth?" he asked.

"No." Amanda smiled. "She lived until I was ten."

"That's a good story. It's amazing how our stories can be so different, yet we are affected the same." He squeezed her arm before removing his hand. "Here, come with me; I want to introduce you to some of the others." He held out his hand and pulled Amanda to her feet.

She followed him around the room meeting other members of the club. Before she knew it, the room had thinned. Amanda glanced at her watch and realized she should be going too. She stopped at the table by the door to sign the email sheet before leaving. No way was she going to miss the chance of getting involved with this group; it was a perfect fit for her.

Amanda glanced around for Jared who had wandered off a moment before. She wanted to say goodbye, but he appeared deep in conversation with Sarah, so she decided she would just catch him later.

As she pushed open the outside door, the chill of the night air shook her. The sun had fully set as the meeting had gone on and now shadows loomed across the open campus. Amanda shivered, wishing she had come with someone so she wouldn't have to leave alone. Goosebumps broke out on her arms, and she rubbed her hands up them to quiet the attack.

WHEN THE CONVERSATION with Sarah ended, Jared looked around for Amanda, but she was nowhere to be seen. He had been hoping to walk her home. Taking a chance that he had just missed her, Jared headed to the exit.

She wasn't in the hallway, but as he reached the main entrance, he saw a figure standing on the top of the stairs. Her red hair shimmered in the moonlight.

"Can I walk you home?" he asked as he pushed open the front door.

She turned to him, a look of relief in her eyes. "Thank you, that would be nice. I didn't realize it had gotten so late, and I didn't want to walk across the campus alone."

"I completely agree." Jared shoved his hands in the pockets of his brown leather jacket to keep from grabbing her hand. He had felt such a tingling sensation when they had touched earlier that he wanted to repeat it, but he didn't know if she had a boyfriend and he didn't want to overstep any bounds.

"I'm so glad I came tonight," she said as they walked down the steps. "This really seems like something I'll love."

"I'm glad you did too. Tracy forgot to mention it, but we have a small office in Holden Hall that we run on a volunteer basis. Mainly we do a lot of planning there, but occasionally the phone rings. We have women who call us first if they aren't familiar with the clinics in the city, and we help get them set up. It's pretty boring most days and doesn't pay anything, but do you think you'd like to volunteer?" He held his breath as he waited for her answer. If she said yes, it would be a great way for him to get to know her better.

Her green eyes sparkled. "I'd love to. I'm not looking for a job, just a way to help, and that sounds perfect. Besides, doing God's work is never boring."

Her words brought a smile to his face. He had prayed so long to find a godly woman, and while he had met many, Amanda was the first one who had sent his heart racing.

"Oh," she said with a sigh. "This is me."

Jared swallowed his disappointment at the large dorm building. He didn't want to say goodnight to Amanda yet. "Thank you for allowing me to walk you home. I hope you can make it to the fair next week." He stopped just to the side of the front entrance and rocked back and forth on his heels.

"I wouldn't miss it," she said.

An awkward silence fell between them as Jared debated whether to ask her out or not. He opened his mouth to ask, but in the end, he decided to wait. Closing his mouth, he lifted his hand in a small wave and walked away.

"Lord, please give me wisdom about Amanda," he prayed silently as he returned to his dorm. "I feel a connection to her, but I want to follow your will."

AMANDA RETURNED the wave and watched Jared walk away. For a second, she'd thought Jared was going to ask her out. The thought had excited and terrified her at the same time because she was also seeing Caleb, but then he'd just walked away, leaving her even more confused.

Had she misread his affections? Did it matter? She was dating Caleb, wasn't she? Of course she had no idea what Caleb's idea of dating was. Her idea of dating was seeing only one person at a time, but she'd known many people in high school who went out with a different person each weekend.

With a sigh, she mounted the steps and pulled open the large front door of the dorm. A part of her longed for the simpler times of high school.

Jade looked up as Amanda entered the room. "What happened to you?"

While Jade was not the first person Amanda would choose to confide in, she had no one else at the moment. "Do you think it's possible to like two guys at the same time?" Amanda asked slowly as she removed her jacket.

Jade snorted. "Seriously? Of course, it's possible. I didn't think it would be for you, you know being such a prude and all, but for the rest of us, it's pretty normal."

Amanda let the rude comment slide. Her desire for knowledge outweighed a bruised ego tonight. "So, how do you choose?"

"Choose?" Jade wrinkled her forehead and looked

at Amanda as if she were an alien. "You don't choose; you just date them both until you decide which you like more."

"I can't do that," Amanda said, sitting on her bed. "Dating is about finding your perfect match. I couldn't date both at the same time, but I'm no longer sure which one I want to date more."

Jade shook her head. "I don't think I'll ever understand you. If you date them both, you would be booked every Friday and Saturday night. Maybe they'll even compete and buy you things trying to win your affection. This could be very lucrative for you."

Amanda's mouth dropped open. Was she serious? "I could never do that. Stringing a guy along just to get presents would just be wrong. Besides, I'm not even sure Jared likes me. He had the chance, and he didn't ask me out tonight. Maybe I just misread the signs."

"Well then, problem solved," Jade said turning back to her book. "Date the other one, whatever his name is."

"It's Caleb," Amanda interjected.

"Fine," Jade said, waving her hand in a dismissive gesture. "He was first, and this new guy sounds like a prude, *if* he even likes you." She paused and looked back up at Amanda. "Of course, so are you, so maybe you should dump the first guy and date the second one. You'd probably be perfect together."

Though Amanda knew it was a dig, Jade's words were exactly what she feared. Jared did seem perfect for her. If she continued seeing Caleb, would she miss out on the guy she was supposed to be with?

CHAPTER 6

*A*manda smoothed her skirt and applied a layer of lip gloss in front of the mirror. Tonight would be her first real date out with Caleb, and her stomach had been in knots all day.

"So, you going to get some tonight?" Jade smirked from her bed.

Biting back the first reply that popped in her mind, Amanda took a deep, calming breath and faced her. "You know I'm not; I've already told you that, and you don't have to be intimate with everyone you meet."

Jade wrinkled her brow and tilted her head. "Who said I am?"

As Amanda sat on her bed, she prayed for

wisdom. She wanted to reach Jade, but she knew she needed just the right words. "You did when you had your tryst here the other day. It was only the second week. There's no way you knew that guy very well."

"You don't know what I feel for him," Jade said bristling.

"Well, it's not from lack of trying," Amanda replied, "I've been trying to get to know you." Amanda bit her lip as she tried to soften her next statement. "Look, all I'm saying is that whatever you're looking for, a man probably can't supply. But Jesus? He can heal any pain you're feeling."

Jade snorted and rolled her eyes. "Yeah, Jesus has never been there for me. I've always had to look out for myself."

"Have you ever asked him?" Jade opened her mouth to reply but then shut it again. A knock sounded at the door, and both girls looked that direction. Amanda's heart sank a bit; she had thought there had been a moment when Jade was going to let her in. "That will be Caleb, but I hope we can talk again soon." Jade gave no answer, and Amanda sighed softly as she pushed herself off the bed and crossed to the door.

Caleb stood on the other side of the door, looking

dapper in a blue shirt that perfectly matched his eyes. Amanda's heartbeat sped up as her eyes were drawn to the shirt stretched across his muscular chest. She turned back to Jade to avoid blushing. "Caleb, this is my roommate Jade. Jade, Caleb."

Jade harrumphed a half-hearted reply, and Caleb raised his brows. Amanda rolled her eyes and shook her head slightly to indicate she'd explain later.

"She seems pleasant," Caleb said as Amanda pulled the door shut behind them.

"I think she is underneath. It seems like there's some hurt in her past."

Caleb nodded and grabbed Amanda's hand. She smiled up at him as a tingle ran up her arm. For the moment, Jade was forgotten.

AMANDA'S JAW dropped as Caleb pulled into the parking lot of the theater. The building was painted a bright purple with a marquis advertising the shows in bright lights. "Wow, it's so..."

"Hideous?" he asked with a laugh. "I know. They painted it last year, and I have no idea why they chose purple."

Amanda shook her head as she climbed out of the truck and walked around to meet Caleb, who grabbed her hand and led the way to the ticket agent.

"Two for Child's Play," he said, pulling out his wallet with his free hand.

The color drained from Amanda's face, and her throat constricted. "Is that a horror movie?" she asked softly.

Amanda had sworn off scary movies at the age of twelve after a scary slumber party. They had been watching some crazy show about a possessed doll that grew until it was big enough to kill everyone in the house. Though she had known it wasn't real, she couldn't shake the fear as she climbed into her sleeping bag. Her active imagination had run wild, and long after everyone else was asleep, her eyes were still wide open.

The house had grown eerily quiet, unusual with twenty girls filling the living room. Then a noise that she could only describe as the sound of something growing began radiating from a cabinet. Her eyes had stayed glued to that cabinet until morning.

Amanda shivered as the memory of the weird sound and the terror that had coursed through her body filled her mind again. The fear had carried over into her own house for another week. Some nights she even had to watch a silly cartoon before falling asleep, so the image of the terrifying doll wasn't the last thing in her mind.

"Yeah, I heard it's great. Don't you like scary movies?" He raised his eyebrow in insinuation.

Amanda felt like he wanted her to say yes, but she wasn't sure she could. Did she tell him the truth or hope her fear had been tamed with age? "Actually, I don't."

Caleb let out a deep breath. "Okay," he said slowly and turned back to the movie board listing. "Well, the only other thing playing close to now is a cartoon."

"I don't mind cartoons." Amanda squeezed his hand, hoping he would understand.

The movie attendant, probably a high school student by his baby face, shook his head but exchanged the tickets.

Caleb appeared to hold no ill will and held the door open for Amanda. After buying popcorn and drinks, they made their way down the purple carpeted hallway to the theater. Where did one even find purple carpet?

The lights inside the theater were already dimmed, but as Amanda scanned the room, she could see they were the only people in the theater.

"Well, I guess there's an upside to cartoons late at night after all," Caleb grinned and headed to the very top of the theater.

Warnings fired again in Amanda's head. Though she'd never done it, she had heard many stories of couples making out in the top row of theaters where the movie attendant couldn't see them. In fact, she was almost sure that's how one of the many girls who had gotten pregnant at her high school had found herself in that unfortunate situation, but Amanda pushed the warnings aside as she climbed the stairs after him. Caleb didn't seem the type to force himself on her. He hadn't pushed her to be intimate, and after all, he had agreed to see a cartoon for her.

He sat down in the one of the middle chairs, and Amanda took the plush seat to his left. Even the velvet on the chairs was purple. She wondered who the decorator had been and if the manager who had approved the color scheme had been color blind.

The lights dimmed and the previews started. Though not a romantic movie, Amanda felt her face flush every time her fingers touched Caleb's in the popcorn bowl.

When the popcorn was gone, Caleb held her

hand, and though he traced slow circles on it that caused her heartbeat to amplify in her ears, he never made a move to go further.

"You ready?" he asked as the movie ended.

"Can we stay till all the credits run?" Amanda asked.

"I guess," Caleb said, wrinkling his brow, "but why? The movie's over."

"I did a play once in High School. The actors got all the credit, but no one mentioned our light, sound, and tech crew who did all the backstage work. Without them, our play would have been a disaster. Ever since, I've wanted to stay through the credits as a thank you to the behind-the-scenes people. I know, it's silly," Amanda said as the expression on his face changed from curiosity to disbelief.

The corner of his lip pulled up into a smile. "No, I think it's sweet. I've just never known anyone quite like you."

When the last credit rolled and the lights came back up, Amanda rose and followed Caleb out of the theater.

As Caleb pushed open the door to the outside, Amanda shivered. Though still summer, the night air held a slight chill that bit through her short sleeve shirt. Not missing a beat, Caleb placed his arm around her shoulder and pulled her to his side. The masculine scent of his cologne wafted to her nose, and a spark of desire flared within her. Amanda wrapped her arm about his waist and smiled up at him.

As she climbed into his car, Amanda couldn't decide if she wanted to be closer to him or farther away so as not to inflame the desire. "So, are we still on for church on Sunday?" she asked. Perhaps if she reminded herself that the Holy Spirit was watching, her racing heart would calm down.

"What? Oh, yeah, church, sure." He turned his head away. "Did you want to try the Experience Life place?"

"That sounds fine. Do you know what time the service starts?"

"No, can you check?"

Amanda pulled out her cell phone and tapped the Safari app to open the search engine, but her email popped up instead. At the top of the Inbox list was an email from the Students for Life. Her heart skipped a beat. Could it be from Jared? She hadn't thought of him all evening, but his face filled her mind now.

Sneaking a glance at Caleb, she surreptitiously tapped it to read, and disappointment mingled with relief flooded her body. It wasn't from Jared, but it was a reminder of the information fair happening on Monday, which she was sure he would be attending. Promising herself she would read it more thoroughly later, she clicked out of it and to the web browser to search for the church time.

"Looks like 10:45," she said.

"Sounds good," Caleb replied, "I'll pick you up at 10:15 then." He pulled into the dorm parking lot and turned off the engine. He turned to Amanda and grabbed her hands. "I had a really nice time. Thanks for coming with me."

Amanda's breath caught in her throat at the intensity of his gaze, and her voice came out barely louder than a whisper, "Me too." All thoughts of Jared flew out of her mind as her heart pounded in her chest. Could he hear that?

Caleb placed a hand on the back of her neck and pulled her face toward his. Fireworks exploded in Amanda's head, and a tingling ran down her entire spine as his lips touched hers. This was so much better than her first kiss had been. *This* was what a first kiss should be like.

"I'll see you Sunday," he whispered as he pulled back.

Amanda could only nod.

❧

"If you're that attracted to her, why didn't you ask her out?" Emily asked as she filled her mug with tea and returned to the table.

Jared sighed. "I don't know. I guess my nerves got the better of me. What if she turns out to be another Nikki?"

"What if she doesn't?" Becca spoke up. "Jared, we know you were hurt by what Nikki did, but you can't close yourself off to new possibilities."

Jared ran a hand through his hair. "I know you guys are right, but it's hard to open yourself up again."

"Open yourself up to what?" Chase asked, entering the lounge with his Bible under his arm.

"Love," Becca teased. "Jared's crushing on the new girl."

"The redhead?" Chase asked. "Good choice. She seemed nice and down to earth."

"You barely talked to her," Sarah said, looking up from her Bible. "How can you be so sure?"

"I'm a good judge of character," Chase smiled. "It's how I knew you had a soft side under that sharp, hawkish exterior you like to put on."

"Alright, you two love birds," Emily said, teasing

the couple. "We should get started if we want to finish in time to get a good rest before tomorrow."

The others grumbled good naturedly but nodded. Though she was the youngest, Emily had organized the weekly Bible study last year, and the rest had eagerly agreed. College was full of stressors and temptations, and the weekly meetings had helped them all stay on track and accountable to each other.

"I thought we'd start with prayer requests," Emily continued. "I could really use some prayers for my new roommate. She's…" Emily paused and took a deep breath, "tough to say the least."

"I could use prayer for my Chemistry test next week," Becca said. "Science is not my strength."

As the others continued to share their requests, Jared's mind wandered to Amanda. He could have invited her here. Then it wouldn't have been so much like a date as inviting her into their friendship circle, and she had said she could use more friends. Yes, that's what he would do. The next time he saw her, he would invite her to Bible study and maybe church.

"Earth to Jared."

Emily's voice broke through Jared's daydream, and he dropped his eyes. "Sorry," he mumbled. "I guess prayers for wisdom."

"And courage," Emily added. "Write that down,

Becca. We gotta pray for this man to have the courage to ask Amanda out."

"I could use it," Jared said with a smile. He was so glad God had brought these people into his life last year. It had certainly made dealing with Nikki's rejection and disappearance easier, and now he had a great group of friends to rely on.

CHAPTER 7

As Sunday morning dawned, Amanda woke excited for the day. She hoped she would love this church and be able to call it her home away from home church.

Jade snoozed across the room, and Amanda wondered what time she usually got up. She seemed to always be sleeping till at least nine or ten in the morning. Slipping out of bed as quietly as she could, Amanda gathered her toiletries and Sunday wear and headed to the showers.

After her shower, Amanda returned to the room to drop off her toiletries and grab her Bible. Jade hadn't changed position, and Amanda smiled at the deepness of her sleep. She had often wished she could sleep like that, through anything, but once the alarm went off, she was awake for good. Even on days she didn't set the alarm, Amanda could rarely sleep past eight. It probably had to do with growing up with younger siblings who were often up at the crack of dawn and rarely quiet.

Amanda glanced at her watch, and though she had a few minutes before Caleb was due to meet her downstairs she decided to wait in the lobby for him so she wouldn't wake Jade. Tucking the Bible under her arm, she grabbed a light jacket and headed downstairs.

"You look beautiful," Caleb said as she descended the steps. He was early. A blush spread across her face at the unexpected compliment.

"Thank you," Amanda managed. "Are you ready?"

He held out his hand, and after Amanda took it, led the way outside.

The drive to the church was short, but Amanda was very glad Caleb was driving as the church was in the newly renovated downtown area of the city where all the loops and overpasses converged. She didn't like driving in traffic anyway, but driving in congested areas when she didn't know where she was going was a huge fear.

As Caleb pulled into the crowded parking lot,

sweat broke out on Amanda's palms. The church was huge, and the parking lot, which appeared to hold close to two hundred parking spaces was nearly full. How many people attended this church? Amanda's church back home had been on the smaller side, only about one hundred people in each service, and she rather liked it that way. It allowed her to get to know people in the church.

After circling the lot three times, Caleb finally managed to snag a spot as another car vacated it. It was at the very back of the lot, so they had a large piece of real estate to cross to get to the front doors. Amanda was glad she had chosen comfortable shoes.

A slew of people stood at the front entrance handing out brochures as Amanda and Caleb approached. Amanda took one, tucking it in her Bible to peruse when they sat down. The foyer was expansive, but the doors in front of them opened into a huge auditorium. Amanda held tighter to Caleb's hand as they joined the stream of people filtering into the auditorium.

Not generally a claustrophobic person, the sheer number of people in this building unnerved Amanda. Was this a church or a sporting event?

As Caleb led the way to two empty seats in the middle section, Amanda's eyes scanned the room.

The auditorium which looked like it could hold a thousand people, was already filling up. "It's so huge," she said as they sat down. "So much bigger than my old church."

"It will be fine," Caleb assured her.

Out of the corner of her eye, Amanda saw Caleb glance at his watch and wondered if he had somewhere more important to be. Deciding she could ask him later, she pulled the brochure out of her Bible, expecting a small bulletin like her church back home had. Instead, it was almost like a college catalog. Every page was filled with a block of information and colorful pictures.

Amanda turned the pages, trying to find their belief statement, but none of the pages seemed to have it. What they did have was a choir, theatre, puppet shows, bible studies, pizza nights, game nights, work out classes, and much more. This church had a lot going on, and something for everyone, but it was so much Amanda wasn't even sure what to focus on.

When the music started, she looked up. She hadn't even noticed the entire band on the raised stage. As the music grew louder, it echoed throughout the room. The main lights dimmed and spots lit up the stage. Though upbeat and fun, Amanda found the music hard to worship to as it felt more like a concert than a worship service. The music continued for half an hour before a man started speaking.

He was ten minutes into his sermon before Amanda realized he was even the pastor as he was wearing shorts and a t-shirt. While she believed God didn't care what people wore, she had always attended a church where the pastor wore a suit or at least dress slacks. The image of the pastor looking more like he belonged at a beach than in a church created an odd dichotomy in Amanda's head.

Amanda snuck another glance at Caleb to see if he was having the same issues she was. His gaze was focused on something to the left. Discreetly, Amanda craned her head to see what had grabbed his attention, but all she could see was a group of college-aged people. Perhaps he was just scanning the crowd to see if he knew anyone.

Returning her attention to the pastor at the front, Amanda opened her Bible and forced her eyes to focus on the words of the page. As long as she didn't look up, she could follow the message without being distracted. It turned out to be a good one, all about keeping the focus on God. As the pastor ended, the band took the stage again and played for another ten minutes. Then the service was over.

"What did you think?" Caleb asked on the walk back to his truck.

Amanda pursed her lips as she thought. "The message was good, but I think the church is a little too big for me. I felt a little lost." She had, in fact, felt like a tiny fish in a gigantic pond, and while everyone had seemed very nice, she couldn't imagine calling the place her home.

"Right? Me too," he agreed as he opened the passenger door for her. "I even had a hard time concentrating because it felt more like a concert than a church service at some points."

Amanda smiled up at him as she climbed in her seat and he walked around to the driver's side door. She hadn't been sure Caleb had even been paying attention, but it seemed that he was on the same wavelength she was. "We can try a different one next week," she said as she strapped her seatbelt. "I'll do a little research online for a smaller one. I also want to find one that lists their statement of faith, because not all churches believe the same things, unfortunately, and I couldn't find one at that church."

"Oh yeah, that's definitely important." He started the engine and backed out of the parking space. "What uh is your statement of faith? I'm just curious if mine matches yours."

"Well, I believe that Jesus is the son of God, sent to Earth to die for our sins. I believe he is the only path to salvation, and that we must have a relationship with him. I also believe in the trinity and the pre-tribulation rapture."

"I'm sorry, I agree with everything else you said, but what's the pre-tribulation rapture?" Caleb glanced at her before returning his attention to the road.

"Well the rapture is when Christ will return and call all the believers back to Heaven. My family and I believe that will happen before the tribulation, but some people believe it will happen midway through the tribulation. That is called mid-tribulation. Then there's post tribulation, the belief that we won't be taken until the end of the tribulation. I just can't imagine that God would leave us to suffer through all seven years. I prefer to believe he will take us up to Heaven before the worst hits."

"I definitely like your stance better," he agreed. "I uh have some things to do this afternoon, but I'd love to hear more about the rapture tomorrow. I'm not sure my old church ever taught on it."

"Of course, I'd be happy to discuss it with you whenever." Amanda smiled at the interest Caleb was showing. There had been a few signs that made her wonder if he were a believer, but it appeared maybe he was and just hadn't attended a church that taught as much as hers did.

They pulled into the dorm parking lot and Caleb placed a quick kiss on her lips before Amanda waved goodbye and headed into the dorm.

"How was it?" Jade asked as she entered the room. She was awake, but she hadn't dressed; she was still laying in the bed sporting a cut off shirt and a pair of shorts.

"It was okay." Amanda returned her Bible to the nightstand and sat on the bed, folding her legs beneath her. "The message was nice, but the church was too big for my liking."

"How did Caleb like it?" Jade asked.

Amanda tilted her head at the question. Why did Jade care if Caleb liked church? "I think he felt the same, but he agreed to try another church with me next week." Amanda stood and crossed to the closet to change out of her dress and into more comfortable clothes.

"Hmm, he didn't seem the church-going type," she said.

"What do you mean?" Amanda asked turning on Jade. "You barely even met him."

"It was just a feeling." Jade held her hands up in

defense. "You know him better, so I'm sure I'm wrong."

Amanda bit her lip as she returned to the bed. She wanted to tell Jade she was wrong, but she wondered as she replayed the morning in her mind. Caleb had seemed less engaged and his lack of knowledge about the rapture was interesting. Maybe he had never gone to church, but if that was the case, why would he say that he had?

CHAPTER 8

he fair was already busy when Amanda arrived the next morning. Dozens of colorful booths filled the street, and a crowd of people milled back and forth. Students for Life blazoned boldly in black on a white banner above a small booth. Jared and a group of others stood either in front of or behind the white folding informational table littered with pamphlets.

"Hey, glad you could make it," Sarah said, "have you ever done this before?"

Amanda shook her head, a little in shock at the sheer size of this fair. She had spoken with people when they had come in JD's center, but she had never been on the front lines, reaching out to those who may not want to hear what she had to say.

Sarah's eyes widened and her eyebrow shot up. "Well, I hope you have thick skin. It isn't always pretty."

A feeling of fear mounted in Amanda's stomach, and she swallowed. *Lord, give me the strength and the words.* Sarah handed her a stack of pamphlets with pictures of dismembered babies from abortions. Amanda's stomach flipped and the contents of breakfast threatened to make a second appearance. With great effort, she swallowed the disgust that erupted in her throat.

"Yeah, it hits all of us like that the first few times." Sarah touched her arm and then took up a position to Amanda's left. Jared came out from behind the booth, and after flashing an encouraging smile, he flanked Amanda's right side. As they were both taller than Amanda, a feeling of protection settled on her from their flanking.

"Help support life," Jared said, holding out a pamphlet to a blond girl passing by.

"Get lost."

Jared shook his head and turned to the next passerby. Amanda held out the pamphlet, trying to catch people's attention, but fear had constricted her voice to a whisper.

"What makes you think you have a right to tell me what to do with my body?"

"What you do with your body is your own business," —Jared's serious tone caught Amanda's attention, and she turned to see a blond girl who looked vaguely familiar, although she couldn't place her face, staring off with him— "but an abortion dismembers someone else's body."

"It's not alive," the girl shot back.

A courage descended on Amanda, and she jumped into the conversation. "Actually, he or she is. At just six weeks that baby has a distinguishable heartbeat. He or she has distinct chromosomes and DNA that is only half yours. The other half belong to the father which is why men should have a say too."

"Every child should be a wanted child," the girl replied, venom dripping from her voice.

"Every child is wanted." Amanda returned the girl's even stare, and the boldness cycling through her blood grew. "You may not want the baby at the time, but there are millions of couples waiting to adopt. They want that baby."

Amanda gestured to the surrounding crowd. "Americans will have garage sales to try to make money off unwanted junk, but instead of giving the most precious gift of a baby to a loving couple who desperately wants one, we choose to cut the living baby to pieces and throw it out with the trash."

The girl stared. Her mouth opened, but no sound came out. Amanda stared back, not knowing exactly what was happening, but feeling power flow through her body. The surrounding noises stopped, and for a moment so did everyone around them. They seemed to fade into a hazy fog until it was just the girl and Amanda.

"Open your eyes and see." The voice that came out of Amanda's mouth didn't even sound like her own. An unseen electric current flickered between their eyes. Slowly, the girl's hand rose in the air and took the pamphlet. At the touch, the noise resumed, and the girl walked away.

With wide eyes, Jared turned to Amanda. "What was that?" he whispered.

"I have no idea." Amanda shook her head, her eyes mirroring the confusion in his. The power, whatever it had been, was gone.

JARED WATCHED Amanda closely the rest of the fair. She had seemed so unsure of herself at the beginning, but after her confrontation with the blond, a new boldness shone from her face. He wondered what she had felt in that moment. Though he had heard nothing, the air had appeared to grow cold when the two girls locked eyes, and then slowly the blond had accepted the pamphlet and walked away.

"So, how was it?" Jared asked Amanda as they packed up.

She bit her lip as she thought about her answer. "It was harder than I thought it would be. Some of them are so angry. I feel like I need to add all of them to a weekly prayer list, but I don't even know their names."

Jared nodded. "That part never gets easier, and I know exactly what you mean. Thankfully, God seems to know who we are talking about if we just pray for them in general. We have to remember that his plan is bigger than our plan."

"Thank goodness for that," Amanda said with a smile.

Jared inhaled deeply as he pondered his next words. "Would you uh like to go get coffee with me?"

Indecision flickered in Amanda's green eyes. "Uh, I would like to, but I feel the need to tell you that I'm dating someone or at least I think we're dating. It's pretty new."

Disappointment filled Jared's heart. He should

have known she would be dating someone. "Oh, I understand. Well, are you still planning to come to the office on Tuesday to help out?"

"Of course," she said. "I wouldn't miss it."

AMANDA'S HEART was troubled as she watched Jared's face fall. He had been so nice and he was attractive, so why hadn't she just said yes? The truth was she found Caleb more exciting. Jared was predictable and reliable while Caleb was… well, she wasn't sure what Caleb was yet other than unexpected. She had never thought she would fall for the fraternity type, but the way he looked at her sent her heart pounding in her chest, and she didn't get that feeling from Jared. Still, she didn't like hurting him, and there was some connection she felt with him.

After saying her goodbyes to the rest of the group, Amanda headed back to her dorm and thought back on the experience with the blond. Though the power hadn't returned after the experience with the girl, the feeling had lingered. That had been God speaking, Amanda was sure of it. But why that girl and no one else? Who was she and why had it been so important?

An intense pressure mounted in Amanda's heart,

and the need to get on her knees and pray overcame her. She fell to the ground near a large oak tree, and the words tumbled softly out of her mouth. She prayed for Jade and for the unknown girl. She prayed for a revival. She prayed for herself, her family, and for Jared and Caleb. Names and faces jumped into her mind one after the other and Amanda prayed for them all. When she had finished, she was tired, but she managed to make it the rest of the way to her dorm room before exhaustion overtook her completely. Amanda crawled onto the bed and closed her eyes.

CHAPTER 9

When Tuesday morning arrived, Amanda rose from bed with an extra spring in her step. Today was the day she would be doing her first volunteer shift at Students for Life. Jared had warned her it might be boring, but Amanda was just glad to be getting connected.

She glanced over at Jade who was still sleeping, her dark hair splayed across her pillow case like spilled ink. Though still guarded, Jade had asked her about the Bible yesterday and they'd had a semblance of a conversation until she clammed up again. Amanda knew more questions resided there, but reaching Jade was like chipping away at a brick wall with a toothpick.

Inviting her to church would have been the

perfect option back in Mesquite, but Amanda hadn't found a church home in Lubbock yet. She didn't want to take Jade to a place she wasn't comfortable at because for some reason, Amanda had the feeling she might only have one shot with Jade. She mouthed another silent prayer for the sleeping girl before she left for class.

Time seemed to drag as Amanda sat through each class. She continually checked her watch, tapping the face to make sure it was still working. Each class felt like three hours instead of one, and by the time the last class ended, she felt like she had been sitting for twelve hours instead of only four.

As she gathered her books, she stretched her sore back and checked the watch one more time. It was nearly one and she had told Jared she'd be there at one-thirty, so she had just enough time to grab a quick snack on her way.

Amanda stopped to zip up her light jacket as she stepped outside. Though still warm, the wind was fiercer today and carried a slight chill. The red, orange, and yellow leaves flew off the trees and danced in the air before lazily floating down to the ground. Her auburn hair lifted off her neck and followed a similar pattern.

A touch football game caught her eye as she

crossed the quad. The guys were covered in dirt, but the sound of their voices belayed their enjoyment. The roar of a lawn mower started nearby, creating a cacophonous noise, and she was glad when Holden Hall loomed before her.

The heavy doors blocked most of the outside noise as they closed behind her, and the air inside the building was still and quiet. Quickening her pace, Amanda hurried to room 145.

Jared looked up as she entered, a welcoming smile on his face. "Hey, good to see you, Amanda."

Relief flooded Amanda that Jared didn't appear uncomfortable around her. She had worried it might be awkward after she turned down his coffee date request, but Jared appeared to have either forgotten it or gotten over it. "Thanks. I'm glad to be here, but I'm a little nervous."

"Don't be," he said. "First of all, I'll stay with you today, but you seem a natural. Also, we don't get a lot of calls, so it might be really boring."

"Doing God's work is never boring," she said with a smile. Amanda glanced around the small room, wondering where she should place her things. A small well-worn tan couch and coffee table sat against the back wall. A battered shelf filled with pamphlets butted against one wall and a few folding chairs leaned against the opposite one.

"Just drop your bag back there and pull up a chair," Jared said, seeming to read her mind. She followed his finger to the back of the small room and set her bag on the squat brown coffee table before grabbing a chair and returning to join him at the front desk.

"So, when a call comes in," he explained, "first we assess where they are. If they are agitated or seem adamant about an abortion, we take their number and transfer them to the crisis center. We take their number in case they hang up before the transfer goes through. In that case, we call the crisis center and have them call the girls. If they are simply looking at their options, as most are, then we discuss the available alternatives and get them set up with one. We can't actually counsel them, but we have numbers we can transfer them to. Do you have any questions?" he asked.

"Not about that," Amanda said, "It seems straight forward, but do you know a good church around here? Caleb suggested this place called Experience Life, but it was a little big for me."

Jared stiffened slightly and cocked his head. "Who's Caleb?"

A blush spread across Amanda's face, and her eyes dropped to study her hands. "Um, he's the guy I just started seeing, the one I told you about. I guess we're kind of dating. We haven't really labeled it, I mean." As the words tumbled out of her mouth, she realized she had no idea what Caleb and she were. Was he her boyfriend? Were they just dating? She would have to get some clarity on that subject.

"Oh, right" Jared said slowly. He leaned back in his chair and looked at his lap for a minute before raising his eyes again. "Well, I go to Indiana Avenue Baptist. It's big, but not too big. I haven't been to Experience Life, but I've heard you sometimes get lost in the shuffle."

"That's exactly what happened," Amanda said tentatively. Why was talking about Caleb in front of Jared so uncomfortable? And was it just her or was he feeling it too? "I'll check out yours then if that's okay. My church back in Mesquite was probably about one hundred each service. I don't want much bigger than that."

He smiled. "I can understand that."

For a minute, they sat in companionable silence then an uncomfortable silence. The phone stayed silent, the office empty, and Amanda hated that the talk of Caleb had stalled their normally friendly banter. She pursed her lips and tapped the desk lightly with her index finger, trying to think of something else to say.

"I'm glad you joined us," he began before being interrupted by the musical announcement of a text message on Amanda's phone. Blushing, she hit the silent button and looked up for him to continue. Just as he opened his mouth, the phone vibrated. "You better see what that is. Someone is persistent," he sighed.

"Sorry," she said, swiping the screen to see two texts from Caleb.

Where are you?

Want to meet up?

Amanda stared at the phone, at a loss for a minute. Though she did want to meet up with Caleb, she was also enjoying chatting with Jared.

"Is that him?"

"Huh?" Her eyes popped up, and a feeling of guilt coated her.

"On the phone, is that the guy?" He nodded his head, using his raised eyebrow as an indicator.

Heat flared across her face, and she knew it must now be the color of her hair. She nodded.

"Well, tell him to come by. I'd love to meet him."

"Really?" Her voice squeaked as it escaped her lips.

"Sure. We'll be spending a lot of time together. He ought to get to know me and the others when they're here," he hastily added. "Maybe he'll even want to join us." Though Jared's face held a smile, it didn't quite reach his eyes, but Amanda took him at his word and texted Caleb back.

Jared resumed his conversation and told Amanda about his life in California growing up. "I just wish–

Jared visibly stiffened and Amanda turned to see what had caused the change. Caleb stood in the doorway, also stiff and cold.

"Jared." Caleb's voice was hard and flat.

"Caleb," Jared said, standing, "It's been a while."

Amanda glanced from one man to the next. "You two know each other?"

"You could say that," Jared said. Something in his voice was off. His friendly eyes had lost their sparkle, and they now appeared hardened. She shivered at the sudden change in his demeanor. They obviously didn't like each other though she had no idea why.

"Amanda, are you ready?" Caleb addressed Amanda, but his eyes remained focused on Jared. "I'm hungry, and I'd like to get something to eat before the snack bar closes."

Neither man had moved; it was like watching a standoff. A really strange, uncomfortable standoff. Amanda looked to Jared, unsure of what to say to diffuse the situation. "Um, okay. Jared, I'll see you Thursday, alright?"

She darted to the back table to grab her bag, hoping they hadn't started throwing punches while her back was turned. They remained in the same position, statues starting each other down. Amanda touched Caleb's arm, breaking the stare and followed him out of the room.

"What was that about?" she asked as soon as they were out of earshot of the room.

Caleb waved a hand. "Ah, nothing. We liked the same girl last year, but she chose me, and I don't think Jared ever forgave me."

Amanda's instincts told her there was more to the story, but she decided not to press the issue. "What happened to the girl?" Pictures of some beautiful blond swooping in and stealing Caleb back paraded through her mind.

He shrugged. "She moved. Back home, I guess. I'm not sure. We just... drifted apart."

The blond vanished in a cloud of smoke, and Amanda smiled. "Okay, as long as she won't be coming back to steal you away."

Caleb's blue eyes flashed, "Not much chance of that."

As SOON AS Caleb and Amanda left, Jared's body began to shake. He sank into the chair and dropped his head into his hands. "Not again, Lord please don't let this be happening again." A seed of fury sprouted deep inside his chest and slowly clawed up his chest. He had to talk to Sarah; she'd know what to do. He texted her as he locked up the room and headed to her dorm.

The warm air did nothing to dispel his anger, and he was sweating when he finally reached her door.

"What's going on?" Concern colored Sarah's voice and face as she opened the door. He and Sarah had dated for a brief time before Jared met Nikki, but had quickly learned they were better friends. Still, Sarah had been his closest confidante when Nikki left.

Jared stepped in and sat down at the edge of her blue bedspread. He rocked back and forth, rubbing his palms down his pants. "It's him."

"Who's him? I'm afraid you're going to have to give me more to go on here."

"Caleb West, that's who."

Sarah nodded, "Okay, so you ran into Caleb. I still fail to see the connection."

"Amanda. The guy she's dating... it's Caleb. Maybe I should tell her what happened. Maybe I should fight for her."

"Whoa, whoa, easy fella,"—she laid a hand on his arm as she sat next to him— "Have you even told Amanda you like her?"

Jared ran his hand through his sandy brown hair. "No, I asked her out for coffee after the fair, but she told me she was seeing someone. I was disappointed, but kind of expected it. She's beautiful, you know? But then the "guy" texted her today and I told her to have come over, and Caleb walked in. It was all I could do to keep from punching him. What can she possibly see in him?"

"I don't know," Sarah said, "but that's not the point now. Nikki made her own choice,"—she held up her hand as Jared opened his mouth to jump in— "and we don't know what happened afterwards. Right now, it's important to keep a cool head. Since we don't know if the rumors are true, you want to be sure and stay friends with her in case things go awry. Getting all riled up will make that impossible, at least until you have proof."

Jared sighed, "You're right, but I don't want

Amanda to get hurt. Is there any way to warn her without coming across, I don't know... pushy?"

Sarah shook her head. "Not really, but here's what you can do. First, and most importantly, you can pray. Second, you become a listening ear. Maybe then she will open up to you. She had to sense the tension between you two and will probably want your side of the story. If she asks, then you tell her what happened with Nikki, but stick to the facts, Jared."

Though he nodded, Jared was still unsure. He didn't know Amanda well, but there was something about her, and he didn't want a repeat of Nikki. "I guess you're right. Do me a favor though. Reach out to her too. I get the feeling she could use some good girl friends too."

"You got it, and I'll be praying too."

Jared knew she was right, but he couldn't shake the feeling of dread that encompassed him. Though no one really knew exactly what had happened to Nikki as she hadn't stayed on campus after the incident, the rumors had flown from person to person. If Caleb wasn't involved, his fraternity certainly had been. Jared knew Caleb well enough to know that he would get Amanda at that fraternity house one way or another, and he could only hope and pray that history would not repeat itself.

CHAPTER 10

*A*s Amanda entered the Students for Life office on Thursday, she was surprised to see Emily sitting next to Jared on the couch. They were deep in conversation, not having noticed her yet.

"Hi, Did I get the date wrong?" she asked as she knocked on the doorjamb.

They both jumped and turned guilty faces her direction. *What had they been talking about? Had it been about me?*

Jared smiled, rising from the couch. "No, I just thought since we had been so slow on Tuesday that we could brainstorm ways to keep the group going and growing. I hope that's okay."

"It's more than okay, but how come I get the special planning meeting? I'm brand new." Amanda's gaze wandered from Jared to Emily and back. She appeared calm, but he kept balling and un-balling his fists, as if he were nervous about something.

"I uh thought that you might have ideas from your clinic time in Mesquite. Plus, you're new, so maybe you have ideas of how to reach new people that we've forgotten about."

Amanda narrowed her eyes. Emily was only a Sophomore and Jared a Junior. It wasn't like either of them were exactly "out of touch." Amanda didn't know what they were hiding, but she had been thinking the last few days about ways to help, and she was happy to share them. "Actually, I do have some ideas." She grabbed a folding chair and joined them at the back of the room.

As Amanda shared her ideas, Jared's and Emily's faces lit up. Wheels were turning in their heads as well, and the three hammered out some concrete ideas to present to Tracy. When the discussion began to simmer, Amanda chanced a glance at her watch and was surprised to see her shift time was almost over. She had hoped to get Jared alone for a minute to ask for his version of the rift between him and Caleb, but that didn't appear to be an option today. She would just have to try to get him alone another time.

Surely, it was nothing important. Men fought over women all the time. Amanda could remember fights breaking out in the High School cafeteria at least once a month and usually over a girl.

As she gathered her bag and waved goodbye, her phone rang. "I'll see you guys later," she said, hitting the call button as she exited the room. "Hi Caleb. Yeah, I'm on my way." All thoughts of talking to Jared exited her mind as visions of Caleb filled it.

The leaves crunched under her feet as she crossed the campus, and she breathed in the fresh air. Fall was her favorite time of the year with the bright orange and yellow colors of the leaves and the crisp chill that whispered in the air. Today was especially quiet outside, allowing her thoughts to roam as she crossed the campus. Everyone must still be in class or partaking of some other indoor activity.

Caleb was waiting when she arrived at his dorm, and after a kiss hello that set her entire body aflame, they walked together to his car.

Amanda turned to him as he pulled out of the parking lot, "Hey one of the people I met at Students for Life attends this church on Indiana Ave. Do you want to try it with me on Sunday?" While it wasn't a total lie, she felt just a tiny bit guilty not telling him the person was Jared, but she didn't want Caleb to say no just because of their history.

Caleb's eyes fell to the floor. "Oh, I would, but I promised my friend I'd help him move into an apartment on Sunday. I forgot we were planning to find a church."

Disappointment surged through Amanda, and she frowned. How did one forget about finding a church? "Oh, okay."

"Listen, why don't you check it out this week and next week I promise I'll go with you." He patted her thigh with his right hand before returning it to the steering wheel.

Amanda nodded, but her previous elation faltered a little. Tiny nuggets of doubt crawled into her head again. What if Caleb wasn't who she was supposed to be with? Shouldn't he want to be at church as much as she did?

Caleb must have sensed the change in Amanda's mood because he turned the car off, but made no move to unlock the doors when they arrived at the movie theater. Instead he turned to her and pushed a lock of hair behind her ear. His feather touch sent her nerves tingling and ground the nuggets of doubt to dust. He tilted her face up so Amanda's eyes were locked on his.

"I'm sorry I forgot about our plans, but I promise I'll make it up to you."

His voice flowed like silk over her bruised emotions and her doubt. She nodded, trancelike, as the familiar tingling sensation took over at Caleb's touch. Her lips parted and he leaned down to kiss her. Caleb's hands pushed at the back of her neck, urging her to respond in kind. As the tingling sensation pulsed and her breath grew labored, she pushed back on Caleb's chest, breaking the connection that was threatening her self-control.

"We'll miss the movie." She smiled up at him, hoping he would understand.

A fire of desire flared in his eyes, and for a second he looked like he wasn't going to stop, but then he took a deep breath, nodded, and unlocked the doors. Amanda's breath gushed out in relief as she climbed out of the truck.

After buying the tickets, they entered the brightly lit foyer of the theater. The hum of conversation filled the air along with the salty, buttery smell of fresh popcorn. As they surged forward into a line, a man yelled out and waved to Caleb.

"Oh hey, come meet my good friend, Trevor." Lacing his fingers through hers, Caleb pulled Amanda over to the dark-haired man standing in the next line over. He had chiseled features though his nose was a little too big for his face. A blonde with long legs and short shorts stood next to him, running a hand idly through her hair and twirling the ends, while her pouty pink lips smacked some gum. "Trevor, I want you to meet Amanda. Amanda, Trevor."

Amanda smiled and put forth her hand, but before he took it, Trevor's eyes roamed up her body. His eyebrows raised slightly, and a smile spread across his face. When he touched her hand, a feeling of nausea bubbled in Amanda's stomach, and she quickly retracted her hand and excused herself, citing a need to use the bathroom.

As she entered the black and white bathroom, she rushed to a sink. Turning on the water, Amanda splashed some on her face and then scrubbed her hands. Trevor's gaze and touch had left a dirty film, and she couldn't seem to get it off even with all the scrubbing. How could he be friends with Caleb? Was there a side to Caleb she didn't know?

Jared's reaction to Caleb returned to her mind. Caleb had said it was over a girl, but what if there was more to it? The questions that had plagued her earlier returned with force, pounding like a raucous parade in her mind.

A stinging sensation in her hands shifted her attention, and Amanda realized they were red and smarting from the scrubbing. She turned off the water, and after drying them gingerly with the paper towel, she headed back to Caleb, hoping he was no longer talking to Trevor.

He was, in fact, waiting right outside in the hallway. "Everything okay?" he asked, handing her a drink.

"Yeah, I guess so." Amanda bit her lip as they sauntered down the carpeted hallway to the theater, trying to find the words to ask what was weighing on her mind. "How good of a friend is Trevor?"

He turned to her, his eyebrows cocked. "Why do you ask?"

Amanda shrugged and ran her free hand over her opposite arm, which had broken out in goosebumps. "Just the way he looked at me; it kind of bothered me."

Caleb smiled. "Oh, he's harmless. He just knows a pretty girl when he sees one. In fact, he'll probably tell me later how jealous he is that he didn't meet you first."

"I guess." The explanation didn't soothe Amanda's nerves; instead it opened even more questions about Caleb in her mind.

CHAPTER 11

"*H*ey, how's your friend Sandra?" Jade asked from the other side of the room. Though still not close friends, Jade had begun talking more to Amanda the last few weeks. She had even asked a few questions about the Bible and Amanda's faith.

"Huh?" Amanda finished composing the text to Caleb and glanced up at Jade.

"Sandra, I haven't heard you call her lately. Are you no longer doing the prayer list thing?"

Her voice held just the hint of a challenge, and Amanda was about to retort back when she realized she hadn't called Sandra lately or Kate or Callie. Snatching the prayer journal off the nightstand, she flipped to the last page. Her eyes widened at the date. Was that right? It had been nearly three weeks?

Amanda glanced up at Jade who had an eyebrow raised awaiting a response, and her face flamed. "No, I still am. I guess I've just been a little busy with class." *Or Caleb*. "I'll call her tomorrow, I promise," she said, defending herself against Jade's knowing look.

"Why not now?" Jade challenged.

"I promised Caleb I'd help him study for a big test." The vibration of Amanda's phone punctuated her sentence. "There he is now."

"Uh huh," Jade said with a shrug. "Well, have fun."

A tiny kernel of guilt erupted inside Amanda as she exited the room. Amanda shouldn't have to justify her actions to the girl, but something in Jade's face sent her subconscious spinning. Was she spending too much time with Caleb?

Caleb was her first boyfriend; it was only natural that she'd want to spend a lot of time with him, right? Jade was probably just jealous because she had stopped seeing her "friend," or at least Amanda assumed she had as the man hadn't appeared in the room again and Jade hadn't mentioned him recently.

Caleb was waiting for her at the bottom of the

stairs, and at the sight of him, the guilt flew from her mind. He pulled Amanda into his arms and touched his lips gently to hers. Warmth radiated through her body, and her head grew light.

"Jade is in our room," Amanda said. "We'll have to find another place to study."

"Let's go back to my dorm," Caleb suggested.

Somewhere at the back of her mind, alarm bells sounded, but they were distant and timid. Ignoring them, Amanda agreed and took his hand.

When they reached his room, Amanda made sure he left the door cracked. Though she was nearly certain she was falling in love with Caleb, there was no reason to open the opportunity to play with fire.

He took the desk chair, leaving her to sit on the bed. After rummaging in his bag, he pulled out a large textbook and passed it to Amanda. Flipping to the marked page, she drilled him on business terms and procedures.

An hour later, she closed the book, feeling as mentally worn out as he looked. He took the book from her hands and then joined her on the bed. As he brushed a hair behind Amanda's ears, a tingle traveled down her spine.

"My fraternity is having a party to celebrate Halloween. Will you come with me?"

His blue eyes bore into hers, scattering her thoughts. Amanda tried to focus; she did want to go, but she'd heard stories about frat parties.

"I don't know," she said in a hesitant voice. "Don't people just get drunk and... you know." Amanda's face flushed and she looked down at her hands at the innuendo she was alluding to.

"Some do, but ours aren't like that. Please." He placed a finger under her chin and tilted her face upward, turning his puppy dog eyes on Amanda. It was like he knew she was a sucker for those eyes.

"Okay," she whispered.

His eyes danced, and he dropped his head, placing his lips on hers. Nerves in Amanda's body ignited, and she leaned into him. Her hands slid up the hard muscles of his chest and around his neck. His hands dropped to her low back, pulling her closer.

As the kiss deepened, Caleb leaned Amanda back. When her head touched his pillow and she felt his hands breach the safety of her shirt, the alarm bells finally blared loud enough to grab Amanda's attention. She pushed against his chest until the kiss broke. He stared down at her with wild and hungry eyes.

"Stop. We need to take a breath," she said, panting.

Ice flickered in Caleb's eyes. Amanda flinched at the hardness that radiated from them. Had she gotten him all wrong? Another moment passed, and then his eyes softened, and he sighed.

"You're right. I just can't help it when I'm with you." He leaned down to kiss her again, but Amanda pushed harder.

"I'm serious."

"Fine," Caleb dropped his hands and rolled off her.

"I should go," Amanda said, sitting up and smoothing her shirt. Her emotions were running wild, and she needed time to think.

"No, don't." He reached out to her but made no move to get off the bed.

Amanda shook her head. Neither of them would get any more studying done tonight, and the promises she had made to herself earlier flared in her mind. "No, I promised Jade I'd do something with her tonight anyway. I'll see you tomorrow."

Without giving him time to respond, Amanda grabbed her bag and left the room. As the door closed behind her, she sighed. Dating was much harder than Amanda had expected. Her mother's admonishment to wait suddenly made sense.

Her mind knew saying no had been the right thing, but her body sure didn't understand, and it was becoming increasingly harder to say no. Should she break things off with Caleb? Though he had always stopped when she asked him, he never seemed pleased at the prospect. What if one day he didn't stop? Would she be okay with that? The thoughts circled in her head as she returned to the dorm. Surely, she could resist. She'd done it for years, and she did care about Caleb.

Jade looked up as Amanda entered the room. "You make that phone call yet?"

Annoyance flickered in Amanda briefly at Jade's persistence and insinuation, but she pushed it away. Jade's advice was needed. "No, I just left Caleb's. It got a little heated, and I'm having a hard time staying strong when I'm with him. I'm wondering if I should break it off."

Jade smiled, "Men are physical creatures. Once you let them down a path, it's hard to get them to stop."

"No kidding," Amanda returned. "All we've done is kiss, but I can tell he wants more."

"What would you say to a girl in your position?" Jade asked.

"What do you mean?" Amanda sat on her bed, curling her legs beneath her.

"I mean, what if Sandra asked you for advice?"

Amanda couldn't stop the laugh that escaped her lips. "Sandra is a sixty something year old widow; I doubt seriously she would be asking me for dating advice."

Jade rolled her eyes. "Fine, think of someone younger. Who's someone younger you might talk to?"

Well, there was Kate, but Kate was her best friend. They shared so much, it was hard to think about her representing someone she didn't know as well. Then Callie's face popped into Amanda's head. Callie had spoken at their high school last year. "There is this woman named Callie," Amanda began slowly.

"Okay Callie. What would she have told you?"

As the image of Callie solidified in her mind, Amanda could almost hear Callie's voice in her head. Amanda sighed. "She would say that if Caleb were pushing me to have sex, then he wasn't a good influence, and that as a Christian he should want me not to sin."

A stray thread in her comforter caught her

attention as the guilt set in once again. It wasn't that she didn't believe Callie; it just was so much harder when it was happening.

Jade shrugged. "I'm no expert in Christian matters as you know, but that seems pretty reasonable.

Confusion tumbled around in Amanda's head. Somewhere deep inside, she knew Caleb was giving off signs that he wasn't good for her, but he was so handsome and he liked her. Nobody had liked Amanda in that way in a long time, maybe ever, and she didn't want to lose the feeling. And he had always stopped when she said no, so maybe he was just fighting his desire like she was.

"What's wrong?" Jade asked.

The thread garnered Amanda's attention again as she avoided Jade's eyes. "Um, he invited me to a frat party on Halloween, but I'm not sure I should go."

Jade cocked her head, and her right eyebrow shot up. "A frat party? I don't think that's a good idea. You do know what usually goes on at frat parties right?"

Amanda pulled harder at the thread, determined not to look up. "Yes, but I already said I'd go." Amanda glanced up from lowered lids. There was a little part of Amanda that was curious as to what actually went on in a frat party.

"I think you're playing with fire," Jade shook her head, "but it's up to you."

As Amanda turned out the light that night before bed, she realized she still hadn't called Sandra, and she hadn't read her devotional for the day. *I'll do it tomorrow*, she thought before falling asleep.

"Do you know anyone in Beta Zeta Psi?" Jared asked Emily at their weekly Bible study. They were generally the first to arrive and Jared decided to use the time tonight to pick Emily's brain. He had heard some troubling information today.

"I don't know," she said with a shake of her head. Her forehead furrowed in confusion. "Why do you ask?"

Jared sighed. "I heard through the grapevine that they have a Halloween party planned. If I can't keep Amanda from Caleb, I want to at least be there to keep an eye on her. I know we don't know exactly what happened to Nikki, but we do know she left right after one of these parties."

"Amanda never asked for your side of the story?" Emily asked. Jared had filled her in on the encounter after his conversation with Sarah.

"No, and I really thought she would, but it's like he puts them under some kind of spell," Jared said. "I just need a way in, and then I can at least watch out for her."

"Okay, I'll ask my other guy friends," Emily said with a nod. "One of them must know someone, and I agree that Amanda shouldn't go in there alone. I only saw Caleb that once, but something about him just rubbed me the wrong way."

"Thank you," Jared said, as the rest of the group filed in.

CHAPTER 12

"*I*'m going on the record that I still think this is a bad idea." Jade said, flashing Amanda a reproachful look.

"Duly noted," Amanda said, checking her reflection in the mirror again. The last few days had been a litany of Jade telling her horror stories about fraternity parties. Then Kate had joined in when Amanda had finally remembered to call her and fill her in, but neither Kate nor Jade had spent time with Caleb. Once they did, Amanda was sure their concerns would fade away just as she was sure that nothing would happen tonight.

Caleb was waiting in the dorm lobby when Amanda arrived there. He stood and smiled at her. "You look great. Are you ready?"

"Absolutely," Amanda said with a smile and took his hand. Her smile faltered when they stepped outside the warm, lighted building though. An uncharacteristic fog had settled on the grounds and combined with the dusk and full moon, it created an eerie setting.

Caleb led the way off campus, stating the meeting house was just across University. As they walked the few short blocks to the house, Amanda found herself jumping at shadows and battling a foreboding feeling. What if Jade had been right? What if someone spiked her drink? That happened occasionally, right?

She wished she had thought to bring her own water bottle. No, that was silly. Why would anyone want to spike her drink? She was just being paranoid. A tiny voice insisted it wasn't too late to turn back, but Amanda tightened her grip on Caleb's hand and ignored it.

The meeting house was a single-story brick house with the Beta Zeta Psi banner across the front. Other than the banner and the music pouring out of it, it didn't look much different from the surrounding houses. As the door opened though, Amanda was surprised by how much room there was.

"We had it remodeled, so we'd have a bigger dance floor," Caleb said, answering her unasked question. "So now there's just a small kitchen and the open space here, and then the bedrooms and the bathroom are back that way."

The room already pulsed with people and the music was even louder inside. Flinching, Amanda resisted the urge to cover her ears. The electronic beat seemed to reverberate down her spine, causing her teeth to throb in their sockets.

Caleb pulled Amanda to the middle of the floor, and they joined in the dancing or tried to anyway. There were so many bodies that they were basically just jostled from one squished position to another on the laminate wood floor. Sweat poured down Amanda's neck and spine, and she glanced around for a way to cool off as she wiped a bead cascading down her forehead.

The front door seemed an ocean away, and they weren't near any windows, but the refreshment table stood out like an oasis just a few feet away. Surely a drink could wet her parched throat and then maybe she could convince Caleb to leave. While it had been fun seeing what a frat party was like, Amanda wasn't enjoying herself nearly as much as she had thought she would.

Amanda tugged on Caleb's arm and pointed at

the table, motioning that she'd like a drink. Smiling, he pulled her close and pushed through the crowd.

"Sorry we don't have water, but would you like some punch?" he asked when they reached the table. Amanda nodded, assuming beer - which she wasn't drinking - was the only other choice. As Caleb picked up a paper cup and filled it with red liquid from the smaller keg, Amanda turned to scan the crowd. She blinked as she caught sight of a familiar face or at least she thought it was a familiar face. What would Jared be doing here? She was about to move that direction when Caleb tapped her arm and handed over the cup.

Amanda took the cup before turning her attention back to the crowd, but the familiar face was gone. With a sigh, she returned her attention to Caleb who held a bottle of beer in his hand.

"Aren't you going to have the punch?" Amanda asked.

He shook his head, "No, the sugar always gets me. Don't worry, I'll just have one." Caleb knew Amanda was not a fan of drinking.

Nodding, she took a large sip of the red liquid and nearly coughed it back up. There was indeed a lot of sugar in the punch. "Wow, you weren't kidding." Caleb smiled and nodded. Another small sip made the drink bearable, and she finished most of it that way.

"Let's go back there where we can talk a little easier," Caleb shouted, pointing toward the back. The foreboding feeling triggered again in her mind, but Amanda rationalized it away once more. Surely, they could go talk for a minute and be fine. There were too many people for him to try anything here. Nodding, she followed Caleb toward the back. Away from the music, it did get a little quieter. The pounding in her ears lessened to a dull ache.

"Whew, is the music always so loud?" she asked. As the words left her mouth, the room began tilting and going fuzzy around the edges. Swaying, she reached for the wall to steady her feet.

"Are you okay?" Caleb asked, holding out a hand.

"I don't know. I feel kind of weird." The room lurched again, and she fell forward into Caleb.

"Here, let's find a room and we'll lay you down for a bit." Caleb pulled her close to his chest. Alarm bells clanged like a five-alarm fire in Amanda's head and she tried to protest, but her mouth felt dry and heavy. She could only weakly shake her head back and forth. He wrapped an arm around her and began walking toward one of the rooms.

Amanda's feet refused to move, feeling like they were encased in cement. What was wrong with her? Her arms too hung limply at her side. Hoisting her a little higher on his hip, Caleb drug her the rest of the way to a room. He opened the door, pulled her inside, and closed the door. Amanda's mind tried to grapple with what was happening. The lock of the door clicked, and fear flashed through her.

Picking her up, Caleb carried Amanda to the king bed covered in a blue bedspread and hoisted her on it. He adjusted the pillow beneath her head and then sprawled beside her.

"There, that's better, right?" he said and caressed her hair, but his voice was off. It was cold, soulless. Amanda's eyes—the only body part still working—flicked to his. Nothing else was responding to her commands, though her brain seemed to be working perfectly, and she could feel the touch of his hand and the cotton beneath her. She should have listened to Jade. She should have listened to her gut. Fear crawled in as the realization sank in that she couldn't escape.

Caleb's hand trailed down the side of Amanda's face and he leaned in. His blue eyes were ice, chilling her to the core. His mouth touched her ear and his words stopped her heart. "Don't worry, you won't remember this tomorrow, and what you do remember, you'll think was a hallucination. You know you want this; I just gave you a little something to help you relax."

His lips then moved from her ear to her mouth as if this were a normal make out session. The urge to bite his lip and knee him in the groin flared inside Amanda, but no matter how hard she tried, nothing moved.

She flicked her eyes back and forth, trying to convey that this was not okay; this was not what she wanted, but his lips just curled in a sinister smile. Lowering his face again, his lips meandered down her neck. The word no flashed in her head, but it didn't escape her lips. Her finger twitched as she tried to push him away, but a twitch was all Amanda could manage.

"Let's see what you've been keeping from me, shall we?" He took one side of her shirt in his mouth and deftly flicked the button open with his tongue. "Nope, I need a little more." Another button opened and a chill hit Amanda's chest. "That's more like it," he said tracing the white lace of her bra. He finished separating the buttons and flung her shirt open. A solitary tear escaped her eyes. His hands roamed her chest, followed quickly by his mouth first on one side and then the other. Then his tongue traced a pattern down the middle of her stomach. "Now, isn't this more fun?"

He looked up at Amanda with those ice blue eyes and smiled before undoing the button on her jeans. Smiled! As if this was a game to him that she had agreed to play. He pulled the zipper down and she squeezed her eyes shut against the attack that was about to happen. Then the glorious pounding started.

"Amanda? Are you in there?" Jared's voice ignited a small kernel of hope inside Amanda, and her eyes popped open.

Caleb glanced at the door and cursed, but continued his crusade. Perhaps he believed the door would hold even against Jared's pounding. A large boom shook the door, but it held firm. Then another smaller series of poundings. The noise hit a nerve in Caleb. "I knew I should have had your friend taken care of."

Cursing again, he pushed off Amanda and began tearing around the room. Was he looking for something? The door rattled again. He ran his hands through his blond hair, uttered a final string of curse words, and opened the window. A glorious thud let her know he had landed on the ground.

Fear and joy intermingled in her brain, and

another tear worked its way down her cheek. The door splintered open and Jared rushed in. Emily was close behind him. What were they doing here? Emily covered Amanda with the comforter, and gratitude flowed through her body. Then Jared picked her up, and Amanda let the encroaching darkness take over.

AMANDA OPENED her eyes and looked around the hospital room. For just a second, she didn't remember why she was there, and then the memories came flooding back. Her fingers gripped the white sheet as the images overwhelmed her, pressing down like a ten-pound brick. The unusual taste of the drink and the dizziness that had come soon after. Leaning on Caleb for support as he took her into a room. The door opening and the large bed filling her vision.

Amanda shut her eyes against the invading memory, willing it to disappear, but it did no good. The image lit up, a movie screen in her mind. Caleb laying her down on the bed. His lips on her chest, where no man's lips had been before, the feelings of fear and despair as she realized what he was doing.

A sob escaped Amanda's lips and she curled into

a ball. How could she have been so dumb? How had she let her guard down so much? She felt dirty and violated, and she wondered if she'd ever be okay again.

$\mathcal{D}$r. Patrick entered the waiting area and Jared shot out of his seat like a rocket to accost him. "Is she okay? Tell me she's going to be okay."

The doctor held up his hands. "Physically, she's okay. She had some Ketamine in her blood, but it's working its way out. Thankfully, it looks like her dose was low, as she seems to remember the incident. We think you got there in time to save her from any intimate attack, but emotionally and mentally she is scarred. She can speak now, but she may not want to. You're going to have to give her time."

Jared's jaw tensed and his hands balled into fists. "Can we see her?" he asked.

The doctor nodded, and Jared and Emily

followed the man down the hall to Amanda's room. She looked so fragile and pale in the white bed.

"How are you?" Jared asked as he reached the side of her bed. Amanda was listless and there was a distance in her eyes

"I'm okay, I guess, thanks to you guys." Though a half smile played on her lips, it did not reach her eyes, and the sparkle was gone.

"The police are going to be looking for Caleb," Jared said, "but they're probably going to want a statement from you."

She nodded. "Yeah, I figured."

Jared's heart went out to her. He wanted to tell her that everything was going to be okay, but he knew it wasn't. He had spoken with enough victims to know she had a long path to recovery in front of her.

"Okay, Amanda needs her rest," a short, stocky nurse said as she entered the room. "You can come back again tomorrow."

Jared nodded, though he did not want to leave.

"I wish I knew what else to do for her," he sighed as he sank into a chair in the waiting room.

"You be her friend, and you pray for her." Emily sat beside him and placed a hand on his arm.

"I know; it's just that it doesn't feel like enough,

you know? I know God is so much bigger than you or I, but..." his voice trailed off.

"Sometimes, it's not about being perfect and having the right words," Emily said softly. "It's about being human and having empathy."

"Yeah, I just feel helpless. I feel like I should have done more to dissuade her from dating Caleb."

"You really care for her, don't you?" Emily asked.

Jared's lip curled in a half smile. "I have since the moment I met her. Is that terrible?"

"No, I think it's sweet, and I think you'd make a great couple, but I'm afraid it may be a while before she dates again."

"Excuse me, sir." Two cops stood before them. "Are you Jared Masterson?" Jared nodded. "We have a few questions for you if you don't mind."

Jared stood, following the officers to a small office. The room was barely more than a closet, and while he had nothing to hide and wasn't generally claustrophobic, the tight space sped up Jared's heart rate.

"I'm Detective Scott and this is Detective Delaney," the taller man said. "Can you tell us how you know the victim?"

Jared nodded and swallowed to ease the dryness

in his throat. "I met Amanda this year, and we worked together at Students for Life."

"What is that?" Detective Scott asked, scribbling on a notepad.

"It's a pro-life college organization. We work together to inform women of options other than abortion."

"And how about Caleb West?"

Jared's muscles tensed as he clenched his fists tighter. "Caleb I met last year when the girl I was dating chose him instead."

Detective Scott stopped scribbling and looked up at Jared with a raised eyebrow. "So, would you say you held a grudge?"

Jared bristled at the implication in the detective's words. "I wasn't upset when Nikki began dating Caleb. I was, however, concerned when she disappeared without a word to anyone after a similar frat party she attended with Caleb. That is why I went to the party. I wanted to make sure nothing happened to Amanda." He stared pointedly at the officers. "I guess it's a good thing I did or she might be in worse shape than she is."

The two officers shared a look before Detective Scott asked, "Is there anything else you haven't told us? Anything at all?"

Jared shook his head. "I've told you everything I know."

AMANDA WAS RELEASED EARLY the next morning. An orderly brought her out in a wheelchair and Jared cringed at the drastic change that had happened in just twenty-four hours. Amanda's eyes were sunken and surrounded by dark circles, and her ivory skin was paler than normal. Emily, who had come with him to pick Amanda up, gasped and placed her hand on Jared's arm. He nodded his agreement.

"Are you ready to go back home?" Emily asked, her bright and chipper voice sounding forced.

Amanda shrugged and looked down at her hands. Jared and Emily exchanged another glance as they walked out to his car.

The ride back to the dorms was quiet and uncomfortable.

"Is there anything I can do for you?" Jared asked as he opened the door for Amanda and helped her out.

"No, thank you. I think I just need some time." She walked into the dorm, leaving the two friends staring at each other.

"I'm worried about her," Jared said.

Emily nodded as she stated, "I am too. I'll try to talk to her roommate tomorrow and see if she knows of anyone we could contact for Amanda. Family or friends or someone."

"That's a great idea," Jared said. "Let me know what you find out and how I can help."

CHAPTER 14

*A*manda walked into the dorm feeling much older than she had when she had left the previous night. She hoped Jade would be gone, so she could simply curl up in her bed and avoid questions. Amanda knew she would want to know what happened and why Amanda had been out all night.

Her hand trembled as she reached for the door handle. If she couldn't bear to face her roommate, how was she going to face the rest of the students in her classes? For that matter, how was she going to face Jared and Emily again who knew everything? With a heavy sigh, Amanda pushed the door open and entered the room, her head down.

The room was blissfully dark and empty. Without even removing her clothes, Amanda climbed into the bed, faced the wall, and pulled the blanket up by her ear. Though all she wanted to do was disappear, she couldn't get the image of Caleb's malicious grin out of her mind.

Except to use the bathroom, Amanda didn't get out of bed the rest of the day or for her class the next morning. At some point, she heard Jade enter, but the girl was eerily quiet. She didn't ask Amanda how she was feeling which led Amanda to believe Jared or Emily had spoken with her.

Whenever Amanda would get up to shuffle down the hallway to the bathroom, she would see food sitting on top of her study desk, but she had no appetite.

AFTER JADE LEFT for the day, Amanda pushed back the covers. She had no plans to attend class, but the ripe smell coming off her body was starting to affect her, and she decided she could at least shower before returning to bed. Gathering her bath items, she walked, head down, to the bathrooms a few doors down.

Though the hot water didn't erase the violated feeling, it did soothe her raw nerves minutely. After drying off and dressing, albeit in baggy sweats and an oversized shirt, she headed back to the dorm room, ready to crawl back under the covers. Her sheets would need a wash soon too, but that was a problem for another day.

Amanda stopped in the hallway at the sight of the blond girl standing outside her room. The girl faced the closed door, clenching and releasing her fists, as if unsure whether to knock or not. Something about her seemed familiar, but Amanda's mind was unable to place from where.

"Can I help you?"

The girl's wide eyes met Amanda's. "Um, I was hoping maybe we could talk." The words were so quiet that Amanda wasn't even sure she'd heard her right. "You may not remember me, but I'm Jordan. We met at the fair. I felt... I don't know, some connection when we talked."

The memory surged through Amanda's mind again. Of course, the feeling of that other voice. "I remember," she said slowly, still not sure why Jordan was here. Why had she sought Amanda out? She waited for Jordan to explain, but when the girl stayed silent, Amanda figured whatever she had to say was important and not something she wanted to share in the hallway. "Come on inside," Amanda finally offered, opening the door.

When the door shut behind them, Jordan turned to Amanda. She rubbed her hands together and averted her eyes to the floor. "I know you're probably wondering how I found you and why I'm here."

Amanda nodded, dropping her bath items on the bed and sitting down. She motioned for Jordan to do the same.

Jordan hesitated, but sat down on Jade's bed across the room. She ran her palms down her pant legs. "So, I remembered your group Students for Life, and I went to their office. Your friend Jared told me where I could find you after he heard my story." A pause ensued as if she were gathering the courage to continue. "I... uh... heard you were attacked the other night at Beta Zeta Psi's house." She dared a glance from under lowered lids.

"I was." Amanda couldn't believe Jared would tell this girl where she lived, no matter what Jordan's story was, but since the girl was here, she decided to listen anyway.

"I was too. Not the other night, but at the end of last year." The girl's hands twisted in her lap.

A cold vice squeezed on Amanda's heart. "Was it... was it Caleb West?"

The girl shook her head, "No, a guy named Trevor. Trevor Jones, but I heard he was friends with Caleb."

Amanda's eyes widened, and she shivered. "I met Trevor. He gave me the creeps. So, this wasn't the first time..."

Jordan shook her head. "I've heard rumors that there have been others too. I don't think the whole fraternity is involved, just a close group of Caleb and Trevor's friends."

A hatred boiled in Amanda's stomach and overshadowed her fear and sadness. "I think we need to speak out about this. We have to stop them, no matter how many there are."

The girl curled inward. "I don't know if I can do that. I wasn't as lucky as you. No one was there to save me. Can I tell you my story?"

Amanda nodded, suddenly curious to hear Jordan's experience.

Jordan took a deep breath. "I was a freshman last year, new to campus and from a really small town. I hadn't dated much in high school, so when Trevor paid attention to me, I fell hard. I couldn't believe he would be interested in someone like me."

The words pierced Amanda's heart; they were so close to her own story.

"Anyway, near the end of last year, he invited me to a party at the frat house. I was elated. I would get to walk in on Trevor Jones's arm. I just didn't know I'd be walking out alone." She paused before continuing. "I have little memory of that night. I remember it was loud and there were a lot of people there. I remember being really tired, and then it's all kind of blank. I woke the next morning, sore and confused. Trevor was gone. In fact, everyone was gone. The house was completely empty. I couldn't believe he had just left me there.

"A few weeks later, I began vomiting several times a day. My clothes felt tight and I was sore everywhere. After a trip to the clinic, I found out I was pregnant. That's when I began to piece together what had happened. I was a virgin before that night, and Trevor drugging me and taking advantage was the only thing that made sense."

Amanda's hand covered her open mouth. That could have been her fate if it hadn't been for Emily and Jared.

"I thought my mom at least would be supportive, but she told me that I needed to have an abortion. I kept putting it off though I wasn't even sure why. I didn't have any moral opposition to abortion. Finally, I decided I couldn't put it off any longer and I looked up the closest clinic, which was in Dallas. I was supposed to be going the day I met you at the fair, but something wasn't sitting right, and I decided to go for a walk. I don't know how I even ended up at the fair or at your booth, but then you spoke to me, and something changed. I got this feeling that I was having a son and that I couldn't abort him. I ended up calling a health clinic here, and I decided to put him up for adoption."

Amanda's heart went out to the blond. No one should have to deal with what she was going through.

"It's not going to be easy carrying this child, especially after the way he was conceived, but I realized it wasn't his fault either. And the center gave me a job, so I'm answering phones there now and helping other girls like me. I just wanted to say thank you. I was so depressed this year, but having a purpose for this baby now, I feel like the cloud is starting to lift. I hope you can find some of that too."

As Jordan spoke, Amanda realized they had met even before the fair. Maybe she hadn't recognized her because she had been so depressed the first time, but Amanda was nearly certain this was the girl she had met her first day of class in the breakfast hall.

Tears spilled down Amanda's face, partly from Jordan's story and partly from her own fresh pain.

"I'm so sorry you are having to go through this. Can I pray for you, for both of us?"

"I'm not really into prayer," Jordan answered, "but I think I'd like that."

As Amanda bowed her head, she realized she hadn't prayed since the attack. She paused for a moment, asking for peace and forgiveness before letting the Holy Spirit give her the right words to say for Jordan. "I haven't really felt like going out lately," Amanda said after the prayer, "but when I do, would you like to go to church with my friends and me?"

Jordan nodded and the girls exchanged numbers.

"Thank you for coming today," Amanda said. "You have no idea how much I needed this."

When the door shut behind Jordan, Amanda fell to her knees in front of her bed. "Help me Lord. I don't know how to get over this attack. I'm so grateful that I was able to help Jordan, but now I need help. Please give me a sign and help me heal." No more words formed on her lips, but her heart continued to bleed out prayers. When nothing remained, she climbed into bed, mentally exhausted, and closed her eyes.

CHAPTER 15

"Should we have asked her first?" Emily asked Jared as they stood outside Amanda's door.

"She would have just said no," Jared returned, "and whether she knows it or not, she needs this."

"Okay, but if she gets mad, I'm telling her it was your idea," Emily said with a smile.

"Fair enough." Jared knocked on the door, knowing Jade was inside because they had planned the encounter with her. Jade had told Emily about Amanda's friend Sandra and sneaked into Amanda's prayer journal to get the number for them. Then Jared had called Sandra, who immediately asked them to bring Amanda back to Mesquite.

The door opened and Jade stepped back,

allowing them entry. Amanda was in bed, dressed though, which meant perhaps she had at least attempted to go to class. That was a step in the right direction, but Jared knew they needed more help.

"What are you doing here?" Amanda asked when Jared and Emily entered the room.

"We're here for you," Emily said, "and you're coming with us."

"I don't want to go anywhere," Amanda shot back.

"I'm not giving you a choice," Jade said. "You've been living in your bed and the same three pairs of clothes all week. It's time to get out."

Amanda shot daggers Jade's direction. "Why? So people can stare at me and whisper behind my back?"

"Look I get it," Jade said. "I've been there, and it stinks, but you can't keep hiding in this room. That doesn't make anything better. Now pack a bag and try to grab something you haven't been wearing for forty- eight hours straight."

Amanda rolled her eyes, but she pushed herself up from her bed and lumbered over to her closet where she began flicking her hangers aimlessly back and forth, as if she couldn't decide what to wear.

Emily and Jared stood against the wall out of the way, unsure of what to say.

"Oh, good grief." Jade sighed in frustration and stomped over to the closet. "Take this"—she yanked a green shirt off a hanger— "and this." She held out a pair of jeans.

Amanda took the clothes and began packing them in a small bag. Jade grabbed her toothbrush and hairbrush and brought them to her.

"Why do I need all that?" Suspicion laced Amanda's voice.

"Because we'll be gone a few days," Jared spoke up.

Amanda raised her eyebrow, but grabbed the bag Jade had finished packing for her. "Gone a few days? What about church?"

"You didn't go last week, but we'll go to church where we end up," Emily said.

"Have fun," Jade said, practically pushing Amanda out the door and shutting it behind her.

"Shall we?" Jared asked. "Our chariot awaits."

Amanda didn't smile at his joke, but she followed them down the stairs and out to the parking lot.

"Can I help you?" Jared asked as he opened the passenger and back doors. Amanda held her bag out, and he placed it in the back of the jeep with his and Emily's bag.

Without a word, Amanda climbed in the back seat. Shrugging at Jared, Emily climbed in the front seat, and Jared took his place in the driver's side. A GPS sat on the dashboard, and he programmed in their destination. Just over six hours of driving time. *Well, this should be fun.*

Jared started the car and pulled out of the parking lot.

"WHY ARE WE HERE?" Amanda asked a few hours later as they passed the city limit sign of Mesquite. A slight tremor of fear laced her voice.

"We're getting you help," Emily said from the front seat.

A few minutes later, Jared pulled into the parking lot of Mesquite View Church. A few other cars dotted the empty parking lot.

"Come on," Emily said opening Amanda's door.

Amanda shook her head, the fear paralyzing her. "I don't want to."

"Please Amanda. We just want to help you," Jared said.

Jared's sincere eyes pleaded with Amanda. She didn't know what they had in store, but they had driven all this way. Swallowing her trepidation, Amanda unbuckled her belt and followed them into the church. Waiting just inside were Sandra, Callie, JD, and little Hope, who was crawling around on the carpeted floor oblivious to the tension in the room. Relief flooded Amanda when she realized her parents weren't here. She just couldn't tell them how stupid she had been yet.

"Hi Amanda," Callie said stepping forward to hug her. As Callie's arms wrapped around her, all the emotion Amanda had locked away burst forth, and she sobbed. One after another, the sobs wracked her body. Sandra rolled over and placed a hand on Amanda's arm and began praying aloud. Amanda vaguely felt the rest of the group circle around her, but she could do nothing except continue to sob into Callie's shoulder.

When the tears finally subsided, Callie pulled back, confusion filling her bright green eyes. "I'm so sorry this happened to you, sweetheart, but it wasn't your fault."

"It was though," Amanda whispered, finally accepting the shame. "I should have known better. There were signs, but I was too stupid to see them."

"We've all been there," Callie said. "Do you remember when I talked about my fiancé before I met JD?"

Amanda nodded. Callie had shared her story with the church and inspired Amanda to be a bolder example at her high school.

"Well, I'd been living with him for years and never noticed how selfish he was, though my assistant at work knew it. I was blinded from seeing the real him by my affection and by Satan. He preys on our weakness, you know."

Amanda's eyes dropped to stare down at her feet. "He was the first guy who showed interest in me that I liked back."

"But he wasn't the only one," Jared spoke up softly.

Amanda looked up at Jared. She had forgotten about that coffee date request. It seemed so long ago now, but she had thought he liked her at one time, hadn't she? "You liked me as more than a friend?"

"Girl, are you blind?" Emily said with a smile. "He has liked you since he first met you."

Jared's face flamed, and he dropped his eyes. "She's right. I have liked you from the first moment I met you, but I was too scared to tell you. Then you told me you were seeing someone, so I kept it to myself, but what happened is my fault." His eyes brimmed with sadness when he raised them. "I had a suspicion that Caleb was bad news, but I couldn't prove it. Still, I should have told you."

Emotions swirled through Amanda as she tried to understand. Jared liked her, but he hadn't warned her? What was she supposed to make of that?

"Look, the only one to blame here is Caleb. You didn't know"—Emily pointed at Jared— "anything for sure. And you"—she turned to Amanda– "were misled. He pretended to be a Christian and a good person, but he was the one who assaulted you. It was his choice, and he is the only one responsible for it."

"She's right," Sandra said. "You can't control the actions of others, but you can choose how to react to them. If you disappear inside yourself, Caleb wins, and I know you are stronger than that."

"You'd better come home with us," JD said finally. "It sounds like we have a lot we need to talk about."

CHAPTER 16

The sun filtering in the windows woke Amanda. Blinking, she covered her eyes and turned her head. The sun was brighter than it should be. The colors weren't right either, and the bed was too soft. Where was she? Pushing herself up, she glanced around the room, taking in the soft rose walls and the landscape pictures. Emily was sleeping across the room on a pull-out couch. Reality crashed back in on Amanda, and she fell back down. She was home, back in Mesquite, with a giant secret she was keeping from her parents.

Sighing, Amanda pushed back the covers and plodded out of the bed. Being careful to close the door quietly, she shuffled down the hall and into the kitchen. Callie sat at the kitchen table with a mug of coffee and an open Bible in front of her.

"Good morning, Amanda," she said, looking up as Amanda entered.

"Morning." There was more tumbling around in her head, but she was unsure of what else to say.

"There's coffee in the pot," Callie pointed and then returned her eyes to the page.

Amanda grabbed a mug off the bar and filled it with the steaming black liquid. After adding some creamer, she returned to the table. Cupping her hands around the mug, she let the warmth flood her body.

"Do you think I should tell my folks?" The question tumbled out of Amanda's mouth before she could stop it. She glanced at Callie through lowered lids.

Callie met her gaze and took a deep breath. "I think they deserve to know. I think they could help you and not hiding it might help you heal."

Amanda's eyes dropped to the murky liquid. The white lines of the creamer swirled back and forth. "Do you think they'll hate me for being so stupid?"

Callie's hand touched her arm. "They could never hate you, Amanda. You made a mistake in judgment that's all. They won't be mad at you because what happened was not your fault."

"Do you think you could go with me? When I tell them, I mean?"

"Of course, I'd be happy to."

JD entered then, and after pouring his own cup of coffee, sat down at the table, and the conversation moved in a different direction. Jared came in shortly after that. He smiled hesitantly at Amanda as he sat across the table.

Amanda looked away, unsure of how she felt about him. The part of her that had liked him initially wanted to reach out and grab his hands, but the hurt part of her was still stinging over his knowledge and not telling her. He could have spared her the pain of the attack if he had just been honest with her.

The anger boiled up and her jaw clenched. How could she even consider dating a man who didn't care about her enough to warn her? But then the rational side of her mind spoke up. Would she have even listened to him? Her hands shook around the mug as the emotions battled in her head.

Emily entered the room as everyone else finished breakfast.

"Sorry I'm so late," she said sitting at the table. "I never sleep in like this."

"Then you must have needed it," Callie said. "Help yourself to whatever you find. JD is with Hope, but holler at him if you need anything. I'm going to take Amanda to her parent's house, but we'll be back soon."

"Thanks." Emily flashed Amanda an encouraging smile before she turned to the cupboards in search of a mug.

"You ready?" Callie asked.

"Not really," Amanda said with a sigh, "but we might as well get it over with."

Callie wrapped an arm about her shoulders and led the way out the car. Amanda sank down in the passenger seat, trying to make herself as small as possible. She would rather be going to the dentist than to her parent's house to tell them this.

Throughout the short drive, she tried to plan what she would say, but when her parent's single level rambler came into view, she still had nothing concrete.

"Just tell them the truth," Callie said as she parked the car. It was as if she knew what was on Amanda's mind.

Amanda nodded and opened the passenger door.

The invisible weight still sat snugly on her shoulders as she trudged up to the front door, but having Callie by her side gave her a small dose of courage.

The front door swung open, and her mother's face appeared. "Amanda?" she asked in surprise. "Is everything alright?"

"Not really, Mom. Is Dad home?"

With concern etched on her face, she stepped back and opened the door. "He's in his office. Shall we talk in there?"

Amanda nodded, trying to bite back the tears that were threatening to overflow already. How would she make it through her story this way?

Her father looked up from his large oak desk when they entered. In a matter of seconds, his face went from surprised to excited to concerned.

"Sit," her mother said, pointing to one of the chairs. "Tell us what's going on."

Amanda sat in the grey office chair and stared down at her lap for a moment, trying to gather her courage. Callie and her parents remained quiet, waiting for her to begin. With a deep breath and a faltering voice, Amanda began at the beginning.

"I'm so sorry," she said as she ended the story, "and I'll understand if you hate me."

"Hate you?" her father asked. "Why would we hate you?"

"Because I lost my way. I ignored the signs that he maybe wasn't a Christian." Amanda wiped her wet cheek with the back of her hand.

"Amanda Lynne Adams, you were a victim. This was not your fault; do you hear me?" Her mother stood and wrapped an arm around her. "Did he..." She covered her mouth, seemingly unable to say the words.

"No, mom, I got lucky. Jared and Emily saved me before he could."

"Praise God for them." A sob escaped her mouth. "I'm sorry," she said sniffling, "this just isn't what I wanted your college experience to be like."

"We should all pray for God's grace in giving you amazing friends, for healing, and for this young man," her father said.

"And for the other victims," Amanda added softly.

"There are more?"

"At least one, Jordan, she came up to me a few days ago, but she wasn't so lucky. She's pregnant."

Her mother and father shared a silent stare. "We will have to find a way to help them too."

Callie had been silent throughout the discussion, but she spoke up after Amanda's father ended his prayer. "Please come back with us and meet Emily and Jared. They drove Amanda here, and they really are both amazing."

Amanda's parents agreed, grabbing their keys to follow in their own car.

"You'll all be back for Thanksgiving, right?" Callie asked as she hugged Amanda goodbye the next day. After attending church with Callie, JD, and Amanda's family, the trio was ready to head home and back to college life.

The three shared a look and nodded. Amanda couldn't imagine any place she'd rather be for Thanksgiving. Jared shook JD's hand, and Emily hugged Callie and little Hope before climbing in the car.

Jared took Amanda's bag, and she smiled at him before opening the back door. Though she was still sorting through her feelings with him, she was trying not to jump to any rash decisions. Their conversation on the porch last night was still fresh in her mind.

After dinner, Amanda pulled Jared outside. Anger still

swirled in her stomach, but the knowledge of all he had done battled it, and she owed him at least an explanation for her earlier behavior. Amanda motioned to the porch swing, and they sat in silence for a minute as she gathered her thoughts.

"I wanted to tell you that I liked you the first time I met you too. I had already met Caleb by then, but there was something about you that I was drawn to. It must have been your genuine love of God. I wanted to tell you"—she looked down at her hands— "so many times, but I'd never really dated. I didn't know if seeing two men would be right. I didn't know how I felt about Caleb, and then I got blinded."

His voice was soft as he spoke, like a comfortable blanket. "It's not important now. We both have regrets, but they don't have to keep us from enjoying the future."

"About that. I'm still processing, and I'm not sure how I feel about you not sharing your concerns with me." Amanda bit the inside of her lip. "I'm going to work on forgiving you and myself, but I might need some space while I work through all of this."

He nodded, and though she could tell the words hurt him, he didn't respond in anger. "I'll be here when you're ready," he said.

The image faded, and Amanda climbed in the jeep, buckling her seat belt. As the metal clicked, her phone rang. The number was not familiar, and a small thread of fear snaked down her throat, but she punched the button to answer the call anyway.

"Hello?"

"Hello, is Amanda Adams there?"

The voice was deep and unfamiliar. "This is Amanda."

"Amanda, this is Captain Griffith. I'm working your assault case. I wanted to let you know that we haven't found Caleb, but we did pick up Trevor, and we found a book."

"A book?" Amanda asked, her eyebrows knitting together in confusion. What did a book have to do with her case?

"Yes, a large black book filled with names. Did you know anything about this?"

"No, I'm sorry. Is... is my name in it?" She didn't know why, but the thought of her name being written down like it was all planned out filled her with fear. Had Caleb sought her out for a reason then?

"No, but the last entry was the end of last year."

Relief flooded Amanda's veins, but only momentarily. If the last entry had been last year that meant... she didn't want to, but she had to know. "Was there a Jordan?"

"There was," he paused, "how did you know that."

A vice squeezed on Amanda's heart. "I met her. She was assaulted by Trevor at the end of last year. I think you may have a list of assaulted women."

There was an intake of breath and then the pause on the other end stretched on. The man let out a low whistle. "I hope you're wrong. There are a lot of names here, but I fear you might be right."

"Are you going to contact them all?"

"We're going to try." His voice came out in a sigh, and Amanda didn't envy his position.

"Let me know if I can help in any way."

As she ended the call, a feeling of dread mixed with relief crept in. How many times had they gotten away with this? How many women were now out there and hurting?

Emily and Jared were watching Amanda from the front seat. It was obvious they had been listening and were waiting to hear the rest of the story. "Drive," she said, "I'll fill you in."

CHAPTER 17

*A*manda's heart raced as she faced the audience that was quickly gathering. A brown podium that held a microphone stood in front of her, and the media was setting up their own cameras and microphones in front of the stage.

After the police had picked up Trevor and the few other boys who had made entries in the book, they had called Amanda, along with all the other women involved. The women had all met at the station. Amanda had been the luckiest. Some had no memory of the night. Some had gotten pregnant like Jordan. A few of those had had babies and put them up for adoption. Many others had had abortions. At the sight of so many haunted faces, Amanda had decided to speak up about the incident, to tell men that what had happened to them was not okay and to tell women that there was help.

"Are you ready?" Captain Griffith asked.

Amanda glanced over at Jared and the rest of her friends from Students for Life, who had come to support her, and took a deep breath before nodding.

"Okay, let's get started." He stood next to Amanda at the podium and addressed the crowd. He began by informing the crowd about the incident, then finding the black book and picking up the boys from the fraternity who had been involved. "I'd like to introduce Amanda Adams. She was one of the latest victims, and she wanted to tell her story." He stepped back, letting her have the mic.

Swallowing the lump in her throat, she stepped forward. "Um, hello. This isn't easy for me to say, but I felt the need to step forward for all the other women I met. I was lucky that my friends"—she smiled at Emily and Jared— "saved me before the worst could happen. I know not all the other women were so lucky, and I wish I could go back in time to save them all. I want to warn other women to follow their gut. I had misgivings about the man who ended up attacking me, but I shrugged them off because I felt like I was finally getting noticed. Your instinct is your best defense, ladies; trust it.

"Also, you should avoid drinking anything if you go to parties. I was drugged by a punch they were serving. The drug compromised my ability to move, but I was awake, watching everything that was happening. To the men watching, this is not okay to do to women. Many of these women conceived children due to their incidents. All of us feel violated. This must stop. Intimacy should never be forced and should certainly not be performed while women can't fight back. If you have been a victim of an incident like this, I urge you to report it. We must unite and fight back against these attacks and the police need to take them seriously, so we can change the culture surrounding this. Thank you."

Amanda stepped back as Captain Griffith took over again. He reiterated the police department's desire to help women and to investigate these cases. Then he took a few questions from the crowd. When it was all over and the bright lights had been turned off, he turned and shook Amanda's hand.

"That took a lot of guts, and I thank you," he said, pumping her hand up and down. Captain Griffiths was the quintessential Texas stereotype. He had a deep southern drawl and always seemed to be sporting a cowboy hat on top of his salt and pepper hair. Amanda smiled at him before stepping down and walking over to Emily and Jared.

"You did great," Jared said and Emily nodded her agreement before reaching in her pocket and pulling out her phone. It must have been on silent as it hadn't even rung. Her eyebrows knitted together as she read the message and a frown stretched across her mouth.

"What is it?" Amanda asked.

"Nothing," she said and placed the phone back in her pocket. "I'm going to go... do something."

As she hurried off, Amanda turned to Jared. "What was that about?"

He shook his head as he watched her hurry away. "I think it's about her roommate. She filled me in a little on the situation when we were in Mesquite, but I think she could definitely use prayer."

"Whatever I can do," Amanda agreed. "You guys have been so great to me."

"We're glad we met you," he said with a small smile, and Amanda knew he mainly meant he was glad to have met her. She knew he still wanted to date her and she was pretty sure she wanted that to, but fear was holding her back.

"Can I walk you home?" he asked, breaking up her internal dialogue. Amanda nodded and fell into step beside him. When they reached the dorm, he bowed and waved a farewell gesture before turning back toward his own dorm. Amanda appreciated the space and she planned to use it to think on the situation and decide what she wanted to do.

"Oh, I'm glad I caught you," a voice said on her right as Amanda stepped up to the counter to grab her mail. Sarah rose from one of the foyer chairs and walked toward her. "Can we talk for a minute?"

Surprised, Amanda nodded and led her upstairs to her room. Once inside, Sarah sat on the bed, folding her long legs beneath her.

"You are probably wondering why I'm here," she said.

"I'm happy to see you, but the thought had crossed my mind," Amanda smiled. Sarah had been the hardest to get to know of the Students for Life group, so Amanda was very curious as to the reason for the visit.

She took a deep breath and bit her lip. Whatever was on her mind must be important. "It's about Jared."

Amanda's forehead wrinkled in confusion. She had just left Jared. "Jared? What about Jared?"

"I know he told you he knew about Caleb, and I know you're probably wondering why he didn't tell you. Well, that was my fault."

"What do you mean?" Amanda asked, narrowing her eyes.

"Do you remember the first day Caleb came to the office?" Sarah asked. Amanda nodded and she continued, "Well, Jared came to me afterwards. He was shaking, angry, and afraid. I don't know if he ever told you, but we dated for a time, and while it didn't work out between us, we remained great friends. Last year, he met this girl Nikki and he really liked her, but one day he saw Caleb and Nikki together. She told him they were just studying, but the next day she broke up with him over a text."

"That's awful," Amanda said, "but Jared already told me this..."

"Just wait," she interrupted, "Anyway, he never spoke with Nikki again, but a few months later, we heard rumors that she had been attacked at a party. Of course, we also heard rumors that she was pregnant, that she ran away, and that some family member died and that's why she left. My point is that Jared didn't know for sure what had happened to Nikki until they found her name in that book.

"He wanted to tell you that day, but I told him not to because we didn't know for sure. I didn't know you well enough to know if you would believe him or just think he was trying to break you guys up, so I told him just to be there for you and to pray." She sucked in her breath and her voice trembled, "So, it's not Jared's fault for not telling you; it's mine." She covered her face with her hands and her shoulders shook.

For a moment, Amanda just watched her, unsure of what to say or do. She and Sarah weren't close friends, but Amanda liked her. Her counseling instincts kicked in, and she moved to sit beside her. "Sarah, it's okay. You didn't know either. How could you? He fooled us all." As the words left Amanda's mouth, she finally believed them, and a weight lifted from her shoulders.

"But I've ruined it for you and Jared now. He cares for you so much." Her words came out in a muffled stream amid hitching sobs.

"I don't hate Jared," Amanda said. "I was confused about how to feel, and I've been working on it, but you just sped up the process. It may still take me a while to recover fully, but I don't have any reason to be mad at him, or at you," Amanda added quickly.

"Really?" she asked and lifted her head. Her hawkish nose was wet with tears, and her grey eyes glistened, ready to release another flood.

"Really," Amanda said. "I was already healing

after the press conference today. What you told me clears up my remaining questions."

"Will you give him a chance?" she asked. The intensity that radiated from her eyes only convinced Amanda more that Jared was one of the good ones.

"I'd be crazy not to."

AMANDA WOKE, covered in sweat and shaking. Her eyes tore about the room, but she hadn't woken Jade. She still slumbered in her bed, back to Amanda.

Her heart slowly returned to its normal pace. The nightmare of Caleb's attack receded from her mind, but that didn't ease the fear. This was the third nightmare she'd had this week. She needed closure.

Amanda had hoped after the press conference that she would have it, but it hadn't stopped the nightmares. As if on cue, her phone began to ring. The number was unfamiliar, and she wondered if it was Caleb calling from somewhere. That had become a common fear with every unknown number, but then reality would kick in and she would ask herself why he would do that?

She tapped the button and whispered a soft "hello?" Her surroundings froze as the words from the other end filled her ear, and her knuckles whitened from the grip on the phone. "I understand. Thank you for calling me."

After ending the call, Amanda stared at the phone for a minute. Should she go? The idea filled her with fear, but the thought of closure held an appeal as well. Taking a deep breath, she closed her eyes and prayed for guidance. Then she tapped out a quick message to Jared. She not only valued his opinion but had other things to discuss with him as well.

Half an hour later, a knock rapped at the door. Amanda opened it and stepped outside as Jade was still sleeping inside. Concern clouded Jared's green eyes. "Is everything okay?"

She nodded, trying to decide which subject she wanted to broach first. "Let's go downstairs."

Amanda led the way to one of the study carrels downstairs and grabbed two chairs. "Sarah came to visit me yesterday."

He looked up in surprise, but waited for her to continue.

"She told me how you wanted to tell me about Caleb, but she convinced you not to."

"I know I should have..." he began, but Amanda held up her hand to stop him.

"When you first told me you knew he was

dangerous, I couldn't understand how you wouldn't have told me your suspicions, but Sarah told me the whole story. I understand why she asked you to wait. It makes sense."

Amanda's cheeks heated, and she glanced down at her hands before continuing. "I wish I had met you before I met Caleb, and I think in my heart I knew he wasn't the one I was supposed to be with, but... anyway, I'm sure I'll still need some time to heal, but I was wondering if you still were interested in me?" The last part came out as barely more than a whisper, and Amanda forced her eyes to his face.

A small grin played across his lips. "Of course I am," he said, grabbing her hands. "Watching you be so strong through all of this has just made me realize how much I admire you even more."

Elation filled Amanda's heart. "Good, then I need your help." She filled him on both the nightmare and the phone call.

When she had finished, he leaned back and ran a hand through his hair. "Wow, well I'm glad they caught him. I'm sure that will help with your healing and your nightmares, but seeing him? Do you think it will be a good idea?"

"I have no idea," Amanda said with a shake of her head, "that's why I wanted your perspective."

"Let's pray about it. God will tell us the right thing to do."

As he held her hands and began speaking, a feeling of peace and the knowledge of what to do flowed throughout her. When he finished, he squeezed her hands.

"Did that help?"

Amanda nodded; she knew what to do now.

"Are you sure you want to do this?" Jared asked as they stood outside the jail. From the outside, it looked just like all the other brick buildings in this part of town—brown and nondescript, but he knew inside it would be very different, and he wasn't sure if Amanda was truly prepared for it.

"I'm not," she said with a slight chuckle, "but we are here; turning away now makes no sense." She took a deep breath and squared her shoulders, and Jared smiled at her strength.

He opened the door and led the way inside, hoping this would indeed give her the relief she was seeking. The initial room was a small, white area with a few chairs and a manned counter area shielded behind heavy glass.

"Can I help you?" The woman, a hardened tough looking blond with linebacker shoulders asked.

"We're here to see Caleb West," Amanda said softly.

"IDs please," the woman said "and sign here." She pushed a log book under the glass and waited for their IDS.

As Amanda signed the log book, the woman perused their IDs, looking from them to her computer screen and then back to Amanda and Jared. Her narrowed eyes stared intently as if she were trying to decipher if they were hiding anything. After inputting the information into her system, she pressed a buzzer that opened the door to another room.

Jared's unease grew as they entered this second room. It was another small colorless room where a male and female guard stood waiting to search visitors. After a quick pat down, they were led into yet another room with several tables.

"You can sit here," the male guard said, pointing to some tables. "I'll bring Caleb in."

"I'll stand back there," Jared pointed to the wall, "so you can say whatever you need to." He wanted to give her enough space to feel comfortable but not so much that she felt he had abandoned her.

Amanda smiled gratefully up at him before sitting down at one of the cold, metal tables. Her hands splayed then folded then splayed again across the top of the table in an obvious nervous gesture.

A few minutes later, Caleb appeared, clad in an orange jumpsuit. A sneer graced his face as he sat down across from her. "Did you finally decide you wanted it?" Jared bit his tongue and his desire to close the gap between them and strangle the man himself.

Amanda shook her head, and though she might have been scared, her gaze remained fixed on his face. "No, I wanted to ask you why. Why did you attack me? I was falling for you. I thought you were a good man."

"But you weren't giving me what I wanted," he said with a sneer and a shrug. "Besides, it's all about the conquest for me. I chose you because you were so innocent. I like them innocent; it's more satisfying when you get what they refuse to give you." His cold eyes gleamed with malice, and Jared saw Amanda's body tense. Even Jared hadn't known how awful Caleb really was. How had he hidden this evil running rampant through him now?

"But you could probably have any girl you wanted, why do you feel the need to take it?"

"Because I can. It's about power. I had it, and you didn't."

At his words, a smile broke out on Amanda's face. For a moment she said nothing, and Jared watched Caleb shift in his seat. "Well, now I have it and you don't. I feel sorry for you Caleb, but I'm not going to let you destroy my life. I'm going to pray for you and hope that one day you see how wrong you have been."

Caleb's mouth dropped open, but Amanda didn't give him the chance to say anymore. She stood, motioned for Jared to follow, and walked out of the room, never looking back.

"Do you feel better?" Jared asked as they left the jail. He knew the fresh air definitely felt better on his skin.

"I do," Amanda smiled up at him. "I was afraid it would bring back the fear, but I just felt sorry for him. He's obviously troubled. I am glad that he's going to go away for a while, but I'm not looking forward to the trial." She shuddered. "I know it's necessary, but I just want to be done with it, you know?"

Jared squeezed her hand in agreement. "How about some lunch to take your mind off it?"

"Sounds wonderful." Amanda flashed a smile and reached for his hand.

CHAPTER 18

By the time Thanksgiving break arrived, Amanda and Jared were officially a couple. As Jared's family lived much further away, he decided to go with Amanda to Mesquite for the break.

Amanda's family had agreed to host Thanksgiving at their house as they had more room and a larger family to move. Jared and Amanda arrived just an hour before lunch was to be served. Amanda made a beeline for the kitchen, offering to help, but her mother, claiming she had it all under control, ushered her to the living room.

Amanda sat on the couch next to Callie, who reached out and squeezed her arm while offering a smile. Returning it, Amanda glanced over at Jared who was conversing with JD. She still fervently wished that she had chosen Jared first, but God was healing her wounds and deepening their relationship. A part of her wondered if they would be as close if she hadn't gone through the harrowing experience.

An hour later, everyone gathered around the large wooden table. The table was fuller this year than it had been in previous years, and the faces surrounding it, though not all blood relation, were now all a part of Amanda's family. "I know there are more of us this year and it might take more time, but can we share what we are thankful for?" she asked, referring to a family tradition they had practiced for years.

"I think that's a wonderful idea," her mother agreed. She looked at her husband before saying, "I'm thankful that we've all met such wonderful friends."

"Agreed," he said. "I'm thankful that my family can all be here together." He turned to JD, who spoke next, followed by Callie, and then Amanda's brother and sister. Sandra's eyes misted as she declared her thankfulness for God's blessings.

Jared smiled at Amanda when his turn came up. "I'm thankful for meeting Amanda and for having a place to go this Thanksgiving."

"I'm thankful that God is allowing me to heal," Amanda said finishing the circle.

The silence hung suspended in the air for a moment as the words lingered on everyone's hearts. Then Hope banged her plate and shouted "eat." Smiles and laughter issued forth and the food began its rotation around the table.

After dinner, Jared pulled Amanda aside. "Would you like to go for a walk?"

"I'd love that," Amanda said. She was still full from the turkey and hoped it would relieve the pressure against her jeans. They threw on coats and headed out into the chilly air.

The sun was just setting, sending out rays of brilliant oranges, reds, and pinks as they walked. Jared grasped her hand, lacing his fingers in hers, and Amanda's lips pulled into a warm smile.

A little park sat a block away, and Amanda led them in that direction. No one was there when they arrived. The swings swayed slightly in the wind, but otherwise the park was still.

They stopped by a green park bench, but before sitting, Jared took her hands, staring into Amanda's eyes. "I'm so glad that you gave me a chance," he said.

"I'm so glad you have been so amazing through all of this."

Jared brushed a chunk of hair back from her face and cupped her chin in his hands. The electricity crackled between their eyes. Amanda's breath caught in her throat as she realized he was about to kiss her for the first time.

She closed her eyes, wanting to savor the feeling of his lips as they touched hers. A spark ignited from the very first touch, ricocheting down her body. Though she had felt passion with Caleb, it couldn't match this feeling with Jared. This was passion combined with love and a feeling of safety.

AFTER THANKSGIVING, Amanda and Jared fell back into the routine of college until just before winter break. Caleb's trial was planned for the week after finals, and as it neared, Amanda grew more nervous.

Though she felt she was healing well, and the flashbacks had lessened to occasional night stirrings, she knew she wasn't completely healed. There were still times when she shied away from Jared's touch even though she knew he would never hurt her as

Caleb had. Testifying at the trial was the right move, but Amanda wondered if reliving the moment would set her healing back.

"Are you ready?" Jade asked from across the room.

Amanda flashed a small smile as she smoothed her skirt. She and Jade had gotten closer after the attack, and Jade had even gone to church a few times.

"I think so," Amanda said with a smile.

Jared and Emily were waiting downstairs, dressed in their Sunday best as well. Though Amanda was the only one testifying today, the group wanted to put on a unified front. Jared stood as Amanda approached and without a word, he squeezed her hand, sending a shock wave of security down her arm.

Amanda used the quiet drive to the courthouse to collect her thoughts, going over the statement again and again in her head. Each time she repeated it, her heart pounded a little faster in her chest. When it got so bad, she thought her heart was going to bust out of her body, she closed her eyes and took a deep breath, forcing herself to calm down.

The courthouse appeared—a large two-story

building that stood out with its alabaster color in comparison to the surrounding brown. The vice grip Amanda had just managed to loosen re-tightened on her heart. Jared touched her arm and shot a comforting glance.

When the car parked, Amanda opened the door and stood, but had trouble making her feet move. They felt like they were made of lead and too heavy to lift. Emily, sensing trouble, came to one side and Jared to the other. Together they helped Amanda stumble in the direction of the front door.

Once inside, the group had to stand in line to pass through a metal detector before they could traverse to the correct courtroom. With each echoing step down the marble-floored hallway, Amanda's nerves wound tighter and tighter, coiling like a tight spring ready to burst.

The attorney, Paul Brooks, met them outside the room. His dark hair was perfectly combed, and he had trimmed his beard. His black suit coat and blue tie matched Amanda's dress. With a wave of his hand, he sent Jared, Emily, and Jade in to have a seat while he ran through some final items with Amanda. Although she nodded at all his statements, she barely registered them. When he was finished, he pointed to the bench she would have to wait at until it was time to testify.

Amanda sat down and smiled nervously at the security guard standing nearby. Was he to keep her from running or from talking to someone else? He needn't have bothered; the only thing she could even think to do right now was to pray.

Dropping her head, she opened her heart and began praying for a sense of peace, for the words to say, for the love of Jesus to be seen. She stayed that way—head bowed, lips moving silently—until a tap on her shoulder broke the connection and grabbed her attention.

"We're ready for you."

Amanda nodded, feeling a peaceful presence descend. As she entered the crowded courtroom, she barely noticed the people. Just like at the fair with Jordan, she felt more as if she were watching herself than that she was involved.

At the stand, she raised her right hand, placed her left on the Bible and solemnly swore to tell only the truth. The jury sat to her left, a mixture of old and young, men and women, professional and blue collar workers. The thirteen faces staring back at her stirred no fear, however.

Caleb sat to her right. Though physically still handsome, now that she knew his heart, she wondered how she had ever been attracted to him. He looked the part of the typical boy next door today in a nice pair of dress slacks and a blue button down shirt that brought out his eyes. No sense of remorse showed on his face. A female attorney with flowing blond hair in a smart black suit sat next to him. The irony of the choice of a female attorney was not lost on Amanda.

Paul began asking questions, setting up the night in question and walking Amanda through the attack. She answered each one calmly though her heart was pounding a double rhythm in her chest.

When he finished, the female attorney stepped up.

"Hello, Ms. Adams, how are you today?"

"I'm doing alright, thank you," Amanda replied, but her hands began to twist in her lap.

She also began firing off questions about Amanda's relationship with Caleb. At first, they were innocuous, about where they met, etc., but then she began asking very personal questions. Paul had warned Amanda this would happen, but the subject matter still colored a blush across her cheeks.

"If you didn't want to have sex with him, why did you go with him into a bedroom?"

"He drugged me," Amanda responded, struggling to keep her voice calm. "There was ketamine in my blood."

"I see," the attorney said, pursing her lips and walking from the stand to the juror box. "And how did he drug you?"

"He put something in my drink," Amanda responded.

The woman stopped her pacing and looked up at Amanda. "Did you see him put anything in your drink?"

"No," Amanda said, "but I turned my back when he was filling my drink, so he must have done it then."

"I see." The woman looked down at her notepad. "Didn't he pour you a drink from a keg though?"

"He did."

"So how could he have drugged you? Wouldn't the drug have been in the keg and affected other girls?"

Amanda had wondered this herself, but Paul had assured her it didn't matter. She only needed to tell the truth. "I assume it was in the keg and maybe they made sure other girls didn't drink from that keg. I honestly don't know, but he knew what was in the keg. He refused to drink it for one, and he immediately took me to the back of the house for another."

"But didn't my client say that it was just to talk since the music was so loud?"

"He did, but that wasn't his real motivation. As soon as the drug started kicking in, he took me to a bedroom and locked the door."

"Isn't it possible that the Ketamine just heightened your senses and you gave him the signal that you wanted sex, but then changed your mind afterwards and that's why you filed this complaint?"

Amanda clenched her fists in her lap and shook her head, sending her red hair rippling against her face. "I could barely move before he took me to the bedroom, and once he laid me down, my entire body went numb. I couldn't speak; all I could do was move my eyes. I tried to move them back and forth to let him know I didn't want his advances, but he ignored them and assaulted me anyway."

The defense attorney fired a few more questions at Amanda, trying to discredit her integrity, but the peace continued to flow around her, and she answered each one in turn.

When the judge dismissed her from the stand, she glanced over at Caleb as she took a seat next to Jared in the audience. Caleb didn't meet her eye, but whether that was from contriteness or something else, Amanda did not know.

At the end of the day, her energy waned from having to hear all the sordid details replayed in the courtroom. Amanda still couldn't believe how many other girls had fared much worse than she had. Though she had met most of them, seeing the actual black book admitted into evidence still hit her hard. Her Christian upbringing made it difficult for her to believe that men like this existed, men who would take advantage of women for the sheer sport of it.

"You did great," Jared said as they left the courtroom. "Do you want to get something to eat?"

Amanda was hungry, but more than that, she felt filthy. The reminding of the traumatic night had re-ignited the feelings of violation, and she wanted a hot shower to wash them off. She declined the dinner invitation with the excuse of being tired, and she and Jade headed back to the dorm room after being dropped off.

"You aren't really tired, are you?" Jade asked as they entered the room.

"I am, but more than that, I just feel dirty. I want to take a long hot shower and try to forget everything

I heard today." Amanda shivered as another wave of disgust shot down her back.

Jade nodded in understanding.

Amanda gathered her toiletries and headed down the hall to the bathroom. Though a hot bath where she could soak the filth away would have been preferable, the hot water of the shower at least eased some of the loathing. The water droplets felt like tiny pellets stinging her back like a whip, but the image of the soap running down the drain made her think of sins being washed away.

After drying off, she redressed and returned to the room. Her pale skin was now a light pink from the heat of the water.

"Feel better?" Jade asked from her bed.

"A little," Amanda shrugged. "How did people do it? How did they get over it?"

Jade sighed. "I don't think anyone really gets over it, but from what I've seen, it gets easier. You start to think about it less. Some women change a lot though, taking self-defense or martial arts to protect themselves. Some hide away inside, but you've got God on your side, and I know with prayer and time, he will heal you."

Amanda smiled and chuckled as she asked, "How did you get so knowledgeable about God?"

"I had a persistent roommate who was a very good teacher," Jade said, returning the smile.

THE TRIAL LASTED ANOTHER WEEK. Both Jordan and Emily had to testify, and it was hard to sit through the story again and again, but the evidence was convincing, and the jury convicted Caleb of rape, attempted sexual assault, and drug possession. He, Trevor, and the other boys who were named in the book were all convicted to a minimum of ten years. It wasn't perfect, but knowing that they would be put away for a decade brought some relief.

"I'm glad that's over," Jared said as they exited the courtroom for the last time.

"Me too," Amanda said, snuggling into his side and enjoying the security of his arm around her. "This was not how I pictured my Freshman year, but I have to say, I think it will be much better from here on out."

"I wholeheartedly concur," Jared said with a smile as he pulled her even closer. Emily, Jade, Jordan, and several other friends joined them, and together the group walked out of the court house and into the crisp winter air, ready to tackle whatever else life threw at them.

THE END!!

IF YOU ENJOYED THIS BOOK, please leave a review at your retailer. It really does help and only takes a minute. http://books2read.com/Whenheartscollide

DISCUSSION QUESTIONS

1. Lorana Hoopes used her alma mater, Texas Tech, in this story. What do you remember from college or if you didn't go, what do you think you would have liked the most?

2. WHAT DID you think of the book starting with something that just happened and then going back to the past? Did it make it more enjoyable or less?

3. WHO WAS your favorite character in the book and why?

. . .

4. AMANDA LOST herself after the attack. While you may not have experienced anything that horrific, what are some things that distract you or cause you to lose yourself?

5. HOW CAN we ensure our daughters don't go through the same struggles Amanda did?

6. WHAT DID you learn about God from reading this book?

7. HOW CAN you use that knowledge in your life from now on?

8. IS THERE something you could do at your church to help inform or love on women in this position?

9. HAVE you ever had an experience like Amanda and Jordan did? What was it?

A PAST FORGIVEN PREVIEW

*J*ess Peterson stepped off the bus onto the campus of Texas Tech and took a deep breath. Though not her first choice of colleges - she'd wanted to get farther away - at least it removed her from the clutches of her "handsy" stepfather. In fact, if she never saw Paducah, Texas and it's one stoplight again, she would be fine with that.

She slung her black backpack over her shoulder and crossed the quad to Knapp Hall. A folded map resided in the back pocket of her cutoff denim shorts. However, Jess possessed a photographic memory and had memorized most of the buildings, on the east side of campus at least. Knapp Hall was a large, though nondescript, brick building of three floors built in 1948.

Jess registered the cracks in the cement steps as she pulled open the front door. They weren't surprising as old as the building was, but she hoped the interior had been updated more recently.

It was not to be. The dorm had been improved since 1948, but it still looked to be about ten years behind the times in terms of decorating. Variations of browns and greens were the main colors, interspersed with a few streaks of gray.

After stopping at the information desk on the first floor just long enough to get the keys, Jess took the stairs at the end of the hall two at a time to the third floor. 316. The closed door elicited a glimmer of hope that they'd gotten her the single she'd requested. She did not want a roommate.

As the door swung open, Jess swore softly under her breath. A blonde girl stood beside the left bed unpacking the suitcase in front of her. She looked up when Jess entered and smiled. Jess did not return the smile as she asked, "Who are you?"

The girl dropped the item of clothing she had been holding and stepped forward, extending her hand. "I'm Emily. I guess you're my new roommate."

Rolling her eyes, Jess pushed past the girl,

ignoring the hand. "Crap. I told them I needed a single."

"Well, they ran out," Emily stated, appearing unperturbed by the rude behavior. "See, I'm a sophomore, but I offered to room with an incoming freshman if it was necessary. Since you're here," she shrugged, "I guess it was necessary."

Jess tossed her backpack on the right bed and glared at the blonde. "Well, I'll be telling them to look again. I don't do roommates." Her hand plunged into the backpack, rifling through the contents until she found the item she was looking for - the paperwork with the RA's name on it. Ah, there it was. Clasping it in her hand, she glared at Emily again, and then abruptly left the room, slamming the wooden door behind her. "Nope, nu uh," she muttered as she stomped down the hallway to the RA's room.

Room 350 was at the far end of the hall, and Jess rapped loudly on the wooden door when she arrived. A tall, leggy blonde with sparkly pink lips opened the door. "Hi, can I help you?"

Oh, great. My RA was probably the prom queen - every year, Jess thought as she shoved the paper clenched in her fist in front of the preppy blonde's face. "I'm Jess Peterson, and I'm supposed to have a single, but there's some goody-two-shoes who has already unpacked her things in my room."

The RA's perfectly arched eyebrows shot to the top of her forehead as she leaned back slightly and took the paper, lowering it to a level she could read it from. "Okay, well, first off, let's try not to call our roommate names." She unfolded the paper and glanced over it.

With crossed arms, Jess tapped her foot against the carpeted floor as she waited for the RA to explain they had made a mistake.

The RA looked up from the paper and sighed. "This says we'd try to get you a single, but that we couldn't guarantee it. Apparently, more upperclassmen returned than expected, and they get their choice of a single first. So, I can add you to the waiting list, but I'm afraid you're stuck for now."

Heat erupted in Jess's body and her hands clenched into fists at her side. "That's it? That's all you can do?"

The blonde shrugged and held the paper out to her, "Maybe try to get to know your roommate. I bet she's not as bad as you think."

"Aargh, you are worthless." Jess snatched the paper back from the RA's glittery pink nails and marched down the stairs. This could NOT be happening. She slammed the outside door open as she reached the final step. It banged against the wall before slamming shut, satisfying a small destructive desire burning within.

Leaning against the brick wall, she pulled a cigarette and a lighter out of the pocket of her shorts and flicked the lighter on. As she puffed on the cigarette, the nicotine went to work on her nerves, soothing some of the manic feeling. How was she going to make it through a semester with a roommate?

It wasn't that she'd never lived with anyone. She'd crashed with a few friends the last few months after moving out of her mom's house, but that had been a necessary evil and she'd been hoping to finally have a place of her own when she arrived at college.

As she inhaled, plans formulated in her mind. Maybe if living with her was awful enough, she could get the girl to leave. What would it take? Loud music? Being a slob? A parade of men? She would have to try them all until one worked.

The cigarette burned to a nub, and Jess dropped it to the ground, squishing it into the dirt with the toe of her boot before deciding to take a walk to calm her anger and solidify a plan.

When she returned to the room later, the girl was still there and had decorated. Red and black towels, displaying Tech pride, hung from the handle by the sink. Pictures of the Eiffel tower covered the wall above a soft grey bedspread etched with a black Flëur De Leis. The girl sat on the bed with a book open on her lap. Ice flooded Jess's veins as she realized what the girl was reading. She hadn't thought this roommate situation could get worse, but she'd been wrong.

"Oh heck no, you're one of those?"

"I'm sorry, one of what?" The girl's brow wrinkled as she looked at Jess.

"One of those Bible beaters." Jess had known enough "religious" people in her lifetime to know she wanted nothing to do with them. They always talked a big talk, but they never lived what they preached. Even her mother attended a church for a time, but dropped it when she met Jim.

The girl smiled. "I am a Christ follower, if that's what you mean."

With another eye roll, Jess mumbled under her breath, "Great, they paired me with a religious nut job." She grabbed her headphones from her bag, plugged them into her phone, and turned up the music. Though the girl said nothing, Jess could tell the music was bugging her, and she smiled a little inside. Maybe this wouldn't be too hard after all.

A few minutes later, the girl motioned for Jess to remove the headphones. She pushed one back just enough to hear the girl ask something about food. *Yeah, as if I'd want to eat with you.* Jess flicked a hand at her in dismissal and sighed in relief when the door closed behind the girl.

Turning off the music, she began to unpack her own things. There wasn't much, only what would fit in her large backpack. When she'd left home a few months back, she had taken only a few clothes and items, just enough to get by. She'd stayed with a few acquaintances through the summer before having to spend the last week in a shelter. It hadn't been that bad, and it allowed her to keep the small wad of money she managed to save up and keep hidden from her mother.

Thankfully, a scholarship arrived her senior year that covered college room and board. No fan of high school, Jess had done as little to get by as possible. But her Junior year, the guidance counselor, who understood a little of her unfortunate home situation, convinced Jess she was a good student and could get a scholarship if she worked hard. The counselor had been right, and the scholarship had been Jess's ticket out of the abuse she'd lived with for the last several years.

Jess pulled out her favorite black blanket, unrolled it, and covered the bed. As she looked at the bare walls, she wished she could have brought some posters from home, but there'd been no room. Her small wardrobe filled most of the space in the backpack along with necessary items. The contrast between her blank, monochromatic side of the room and the other girl's pride-filled side was nauseating and slightly comical.

An audible rumbling in her stomach sounded, and Jess realized she was hungry after all, but she had no idea which dorm the blonde saint had gone to. Knapp Hall didn't have a full cafeteria, but many of the nearby dorms did. As she didn't want to risk running into her, Jess decided it was time to see what the town offered.

University Avenue lay to the east, and she trekked that direction having seen a few restaurants from the bus when she arrived earlier. The sun still shone, though it was nearing dusk, and beads of sweat trickled down one side of her neck. She had shaved the other side hoping to deter her stepfather's advances, but it hadn't worked. However, it seemed to fit well with her "don't mess with me" attitude, so she'd kept it.

She crossed University at a crosswalk and debated. A pizza place, a burger joint, and a pancake house dotted the row of buildings. Not feeling much like breakfast or a greasy pizza, Jess opted for the burger joint, Ollie's.

The red and black building oozed Tech pride, and a picture of Ollie, a white dog with a black patch over one eye and a red bandana, completed the sign. Jess sighed at the gimmicky exterior, but figured the food couldn't be too bad. It was rather hard to mess up a burger and fries.

As she opened the door, second thoughts flooded her mind. She might as well have walked into an updated version of Cheers. Huge television screens adorned the walls. Booths covered in red vinyl hugged the large windows, and a few tables and chairs crowded a large bar. A lively group filled the room, including a group of jocks at the nearest table cheering at the big screens. Pretty, blonde girls in designer clothes sat at another table tapping away on their expensive cell phones. If there were two things Jess couldn't stand, it was jocks and Barbies.

She paused, hand on the door, and debated her options. Though not her scene, she was hungry, and there were a few empty booths. The renewed rumbling of her stomach finalized the decision, and with a clenched jaw, she crossed to a nearby empty booth. Why couldn't she be old enough to sit at the bar and order a stiff tequila drink?

She'd been drinking since the age of fourteen when she'd found the liquor in her mother's stash. The first swig had been awful, but she'd found after that the lightheaded sensation helped her forget the leers and touches of her stepfather. Jess wouldn't say she had acquired a taste for the liquor, but she had developed an appreciation to the mindless bliss it offered.

A college-aged waiter, clad in a white t-shirt, shorts, and bored expression arrived shortly and handed her a menu. New fears of the quality of the food deepened as the sticky menu ripped open with a squelching sound. Swallowing her disgust, Jess ordered a burger, fries, and a diet coke.

As the waiter turned away and headed to the kitchen, a large male slid in the booth across from her. With his short brown hair and broad shoulders, he looked very much like all the other jocks at the nearby table. A quick glance that direction confirmed her suspicion as the whole table had their eyes glued Jess's direction. The guy wasn't bad looking, but Jess held no love for jocks. Perhaps if she could give him a cold enough stare he would leave, but alas he opened his mouth, and at the sound of his thick southern drawl, Jess felt IQ points trickle out of her head.

"I haven't seen you 'round here before," the behemoth said. "I'm Randy. I'm a linebacker."

Though Jess watched football - she was, in fact, a closet Dallas Cowboys fan - she had no intention of letting this dolt know it.

"That's nice," she said sweetly, plastering a fake smile on her face, "now get out of my booth." The last words dripped with venom as her smile dropped and she glared daggers at him.

Randy held up his hands in defense. "Whoa, no need to be rude now. I just thought I'd say hi."

"Hi, now please leave."

"Whatever." He unfolded himself from the booth and lumbered back to his friends who cheered and clapped.

Jess rolled her eyes and sighed. Maybe she should have ordered in. She turned her attention out the window, and as she watched the cars pass, she wished for a different life. Thankfully, the table of jocks decided she wasn't worth any more trouble and left her alone.

A few moments later, her plate of greasy food

arrived. Jess hadn't thought a restaurant could mess up a burger and fries, but she had been wrong. There was so much sauce on the burger that the bun had begun to disintegrate, and she was forced to eat the patty with a fork. The fries had evidently sat in the fryer a little too long as they were no longer a golden yellow, but an odd rusty brownish color. She could make a scene—demand a refund—but she wanted no more attention tonight. Better to just let it be and mark this as a place to never revisit. She shoveled down what little she could to satisfy the rumbling, paid the tab, and left. It was still better than home, she reminded herself as she stepped out into the humid night.

"Hey, you got a light?"

The voice came from the right where a guy with dark hair and a black leather jacket stood. Stubble covered his chin, making his blue eyes shine like a beacon in a dark storm, and the hint of a tattoo peeked over his collar. Jess's breath caught as her heart hammered in her chest. He reminded her of Adrian Paul's Highlander, a show that had originally aired before her time but that she had fallen in love with when re-runs began.

She nodded, forcing her voice to stay cool as she reached for her lighter. A slight tremor gripped her hand as she held it out, but he didn't seem to notice. He lit his cigarette and then handed the lighter back. Jess shook out her own cigarette and lit up next to him.

"What's your name?" he asked, nodding at her and taking a deep breath of smoke. It curled out of his thin lips in little wisps. Jess had never wanted to be a cigarette so badly.

"Jess. You?" She breathed in a deep lungful, careful not to overdo it. A coughing fit in front of this Adonis would be mortifying.

"Chad. You go to Tech?"

"Yeah, I just got here."

He nodded again and continued puffing. Jess watched as his hand rose to his mouth and lowered to his side in a rhythmic motion, and she wondered what the stubble on his face would feel like against her cheek. Would it be rough like sandpaper or was it softer? A heat seared across her face, and she turned away.

"Well, I guess I'll see you around." He finished his cigarette, flicked it on the ground, and then mounted a black Harley Davidson parked at the curb. His bad boy quotient rose even higher, and her heart pounded faster as she envisioned herself climbing on the back and wrapping her arms around his waist, the smell of his leather jacket tickling her nose.

As the engine roared to life, the image vanished, and the pounding in her heart slowed. He flicked a mock salute and rode away. Sighing, Jess finished her cigarette and began the trek back to the dorm room.

When the building came into view, her good mood faded away. If only she didn't have the perky roommate to put up with.

With a sigh, she pushed open the door to the shared room. Emily looked up from her book, but said nothing. Crossing to the little sink, Jess brushed her teeth, changed into her sleeping attire of a long t-shirt, and then flicked off the overhead light.

"Excuse me, but I was reading." Emily's voice held a note of annoyance, and Jess smiled to herself in the darkness.

"And now you're not," she retorted.

A sigh carried across the room, followed by the sound of rummaging around in a drawer. There was a click, and a little book light came on. Jess should have known Emily would be a prepared little Girl Scout. She rolled her eyes and turned to face the wall. Score one for the annoying blonde, but there was always tomorrow. She would just have to be more creative.

As CHAD TURNED off the motorcycle and dismounted, his mind revisited the raven-haired girl. With one side or her hair shaved and a nose ring, she was definitely trying to portray a tough exterior, but though he hadn't spoken with her long, he had sensed a sadness in her eyes. It was the same sadness he often saw reflected in his mirror, and he wondered what hurt resided in her past.

He hadn't always been into analyzing people. When he'd first come to Texas Tech, it had been to major in Mechanical Engineering, but two years ago his younger brother had been killed in a school shooting and everything had changed. Chad had turned from mechanical engineering to psychology, desperate for answers as to why people acted the way they did. He still wasn't sure what he planned to do with the degree, but if he could save even one person from going through the fate Kyle had or dealing with the aftermath as he was having to, it would be worth it.

He flicked on the light of his small apartment-like dorm room and sighed. The benefit of being a Junior was that he could live in West Village, but as he'd opted for a single apartment this year, the downfall was that loneliness often crept in.

Chad thought about calling one of his "hook-ups," but it would be his first day teaching tomorrow. His time would be better spent making sure he was prepared as he needed to keep this job to afford his housing. Besides, he was rather tired of last year's offerings. Hopefully, this year would wield some new and exciting flavors.

Again the girl from earlier flashed into his mind. She had been attracted to him. He had seen it in her face before she turned away, and she might be interesting. At least interesting enough for some good times. It was too bad he hadn't gotten her number. Tech was a big campus and the chances he would see her again were small.

He pushed the thoughts of her from his mind and focused on arranging his papers and rehearsing his lecture. Tomorrow would be soon enough to focus on finding new women to add to his list.

Click here to continue reading A Past Forgiven

ABOUT THE AUTHOR

Lorana Hoopes is an inspirational author originally from Texas but now living in the PNW with her husband and three children. When not writing, she can be seen kickboxing at the gym, singing, or acting on stage. One day, she hopes to retire from teaching and write full time.

If you enjoyed this story, be sure to check out Lorana's other books.

When Love Returns
    Once Upon a Star
    Love Conquers All
    Where It All Began
    The Power of Prayer
    When Hearts Collide
    A Past Forgiven
    The Billionaire's Secret
    Brush with a Billionaire
    The Billionaire's Christmas Miracle
    The Billionaire's Cowboy Groom
    Lawfully Matched
    Lawfully Justified
    The Scarlet Wedding
    Lawfully Redeemed
    Lawfully Pursued
    The Still Small Voice

Love Renewed

When Love Returns

Once Upon a Star

Love Conquers All

The Cowboy's Reality Bride

The Reality Bride's Baby

Her children's early reader chapter book series:

The Wishing Stone #1: Dangerous Dinosaur

The Wishing Stone #2: Dragon Dilemma

The Wishing Stone #3: Mesmerizing Mermaids

The Wishing Stone #4: Pyramid Puzzles

The Wishing Stone Inspirations #1: Mary's Miracle

To see a list of all her books

authorloranahoopes.com

loranahoopes@gmail.com